Assisted

Living

Assisted Living

Book Two of EarthCent Universe

Foner Books

ISBN 978-1-948691-21-5

Copyright 2019 by E. M. Foner

Northampton, Massachusetts

One

"You don't have to scrub so hard," Harry told his assistant. "Let the pan soak overnight and that Sheezle bug residue will dissolve on its own."

"Where did you learn about all this alien stuff?" Bill asked, letting the pan drop to the bottom of the double sink. "I left Earth almost a year before you did, but you're the one who's always explaining things to me."

"Cleaning the crud off baking pans doesn't require advanced alien technology, and everything I teach you is based on my experience running a bakery back on Earth. I'd like to think I have something to show for the fact that I've been alive almost fifty years longer than you have. Everything takes time."

"I don't know. I like working with you in the kitchen and with Razood in the blacksmith shop, but the other day he told me that Frunge apprentices are expected to assist for seven years before they're allowed to forge something on their own. I'll be old by then."

Harry laughed. "You'll still be in your twenties. Come down to our independent living cooperative for movie night and I'll show you what old means."

"What's a movie?"

"Like an immersive, but without the holograms or the sensory input."

"You mean like the advertisements Flower runs on the display panels in the corridors?"

"Exactly, but longer, and the stories are usually better than commercials. Jack got us started on watching movies that were made on Earth nearly two centuries ago. They're so old that the color has faded out."

"They were filmed in black and white," Flower interrupted by way of a speaker grille in the ceiling. "Don't teach the boy wrong."

"Why didn't they use colors?" Bill asked.

"At first because they didn't know how, and for decades after that, because it was too expensive," the Dollnick AI explained. "And I should point out that working for Razood wasn't my idea."

"He's a great guy, for an alien spy, I mean."

"If your goal in life is to be a blacksmith's assistant for a twenty-one-year apprenticeship and then to set up your own forge, it makes perfect sense to continue working there. But Razood only earns a living thanks to a generous stipend from the sponsors of Colonial Jeevesburg. I'm sure you've noticed that most of his customers are actually from the other species."

"Flower has a point," Harry said. "You know that the Frunge live much longer than we do, and Razood probably doesn't realize that within a few years you'll be a father with your own responsibilities. That Julie girl seems nice."

"We're just friends," Bill said, feeling his face grow warm. "I mean, we went on a sort of a date in the amusement park last weekend, but I got motion sick and threw up on her new sneakers. I've been going to work early and doing my calisthenics at the blacksmith shop so I don't have to face her in the corridor."

Harry laughed again and put a hand on his assistant's shoulder. "Women don't care about things like a little vomiting. They want a man who is confident and listens to them. Hiding from her is the worst thing you can do."

"Harry's right," the Dollnick AI said. "That's why I've decided to make you a partner in my new business."

"What?" Bill looked back and forth between Harry and the ceiling. "What new business?"

"Package delivery. You'll be the junior partner."

"I don't know anything about package delivery."

"Pick up that oven mitt and hand it to Harry," Flower ordered. Bill followed the instructions and gave his boss the oven mitt. "Now you're a package delivery expert," the ship's AI continued. "The rest is back-office work and shipping, two fields in which I excel."

"I know you're usually right about stuff, Flower, but learning to be a blacksmith has got to be more interesting than handing people packages."

"It will be your own business—our own business. In addition to earning real money, I'll teach you about marketing, cash-flow management, customer service, scheduling—everything you need to be an entrepreneur."

"Would I have to quit my part-time jobs working here and with Razood?"

"Not immediately. I'm planning a soft launch so it will take a while for the business to scale up."

"Can I think about it?" Bill asked.

"I'm not seeing the executive decision-making ability I expected," Flower replied. On receiving no response, the AI added, "Julie will be impressed if you go into business with me."

"All right, already. When do I start?"

"At the next stop. I'm about to begin running ads on Bits where we'll undercut the established package delivery services by fifty percent, so we should get plenty of customers."

"What are you going to name it?" Harry asked, recalling how the Dollnick AI had ignored the voting process for the independent living cooperative he was a member of to name it Flower's Paradise.

"Next Stop Deliveries. What do you think?"

"Catchy. How did you come up with that one?"

"It's literal. We'll be delivering packages to the next stop. That's the secret of my business model."

"You mean we're starting a package delivery service that only delivers to one place?" Bill asked skeptically.

"One place at a time," Flower corrected him. "In cases where the shipper can afford to be patient, I'll be happy to store the packages for free as long as they're going to a later stop on our circuit. I expect we'll get some commodities business that way."

"What are commodities?"

"Lumber, ore, cereal crops. I plan to start a furniture-moving service as well. There's great synergy with the ads I'm already running for the independent living cooperative."

"How so?" Harry asked.

"Ever since the Galactic Free Press published the first article about your group getting scammed and starting your own independent living cooperative, I've noticed that most of the queries about joining include questions about moving personal belongings. It's surprising to me how much junk your people can accumulate in such short lifetimes."

"Maybe we're trying to compensate."

"You're doing a good job of it. If you can dispense with Bill's help for the rest of the day, I'd like to take him down to Deck Three and show him the area I've set aside for the new business."

"Isn't Deck Three used by the distillery?" Bill asked. "I remember drinking something at *The Spoon* that tasted like paint thinner."

"You're thinking of Deck Three vodka," the AI said. "It's distilled on the water treatment deck, between the filtration system and solid-waste processing digesters. I like keeping all of the stinky businesses in one area, but my Stryx mentor cautioned me against using 'sewage' in liquor branding."

"Glad I don't drink," Harry said. "Sure, take him. I was going to spend the afternoon experimenting with recipes from the new All Species Cookbook and I'm a bit self-conscious about making anything new with somebody looking over my shoulder."

"Keep an eye out for any baked goods with a long shelf life."

"Another business idea?"

"You probably heard that your former co-species, the Alts, have joined the Vergallian Empire. Their ecosystem was transplanted from Earth when the Stryx moved them to their own planet, so their agriculture is largely compatible with Human digestion."

"Isn't that good?"

"It's terrible. When I began this mission three years ago, I converted a substantial part of my own agricultural capacity to your crops and fruiting trees in order to cash in on visits to Human colonies that haven't ramped up production of fresh food. With competent business management from Vergallian royals, the Alts will be in direct competition with me."

"Can't you just plant something else?" Bill asked.

"Crop rotation in space isn't as simple as you might think, and I have several decks of fruit trees that I started from seeds to save money, so they're just beginning to produce. The orchards that supply your current needs were transplanted as young trees."

"Are you running out of money?" Bill asked. "Is that why you're starting new businesses?"

"My legal proceedings are costing somewhat more than the initial estimates," Flower admitted. "Now hop in the nearest lift tube and we'll get started."

Bill left the kitchen through the small cafeteria that the Dollnick AI had set aside for aliens traveling by themselves and entered the nearest lift tube. The capsule barely got started before it stopped again, and the doors opened on a familiar corridor.

"This isn't Deck Three," Bill observed. "Am I going to the library to see Julie?"

"Julie's internship is in the mornings, just like your apprenticeship with Razood. You're here to see the Farling doctor."

"What did I do now?"

"It's not a punishment. If we're going to be working together you'll need an implant. I can't be discussing business with you over the nearest speaker grille when anybody might be listening in."

"How much is this going to cost?" Bill asked cautiously.

"Nothing, it's a loaner. If we dissolve our partnership, I'll take it back."

Bill approached the familiar door to the med bay, which slid open when he drew near. He passed through the entry scanners, and not seeing the giant beetle anywhere, called, "Hello?"

"He'll be with you in a minute," Flower announced. "Try practicing the eye chart while you're waiting."

"There's nothing wrong with my eyes."

"That wasn't the doctor's conclusion the last time you were here."

"But it's in some alien language I can't read."

"All the more reason to practice."

While Bill was trying to make sense of this latest piece of advice, the padded top of the examination table began to go up with a creaking noise, and a giant beetle emerged from the hidden cavity like a vampire rising from his coffin.

"Did somebody beat you up again?" the Farling doctor rubbed out on his speaking legs. "I don't see Julie with you so I assume you're here for yourself."

"I brought him, M793qK," Flower announced. "We're going into business together and I want you to give him an implant."

"We're already in business together," the doctor said.

"Not us—Bill and myself. We're starting a package delivery service."

"Let's see. I removed an implant from a woman who was complaining about headaches just before I left for my all-too-brief visit to Union Station. That implant is probably still in the medical waste bin if your bot didn't take out the trash last week."

"No way," Bill said. "You're not putting a second-hand implant in my brain."

"I'll rinse it off first," the doctor offered, rummaging through a cabinet and pulling out a bottle of Deck Three vodka. "This will kill the germs."

"He's teasing you," Flower reassured the young man, who had begun backing towards the door. "Give him the same type of implant you gave Julie, Doctor."

"A high-grade unit with the separate subvocalization pickup? You can explain to me what makes him so valuable as a business partner while he's under the anesthetic."

"You're going to knock me out?" Bill asked.

"I could do that too," the doctor said, retrieving a heavy mallet from a drawer of tools. "Lie down on the table first so I don't have to pick you up."

"You're scaring him now," Flower scolded. "I'm not going to allow M793qK to hit you with a hammer, Bill. Just lie down on the table."

The Farling made a show of reluctance putting away the mallet, and then growing impatient with Bill's hesitation, picked the young man up and deposited him on the operating table.

"This isn't going to hurt me a bit," the doctor continued, pushing Bill's head down. "How long can you hold your breath?"

"I don't know. Thirty seconds?"

"Start now, and in thirty-one seconds, I'll operate."

Bill reflexively took a deep breath and began to hold it, but he watched carefully to make sure that the mallet didn't reappear. The beetle retrieved a sealed plastic envelope from an organizer with a hundred little drawers that looked like it belonged in a home workshop and waved it in front of the patient.

"Brand new merchandise. Only the best for paying customers. Are you unconscious yet?"

"No," Bill exhaled. "Was that really supposed to work?"

"Holding your breath until you pass out? It will be the first time for me if it does." The doctor tore open the

8

plastic package and used a giant pair of tweezers to transfer the smaller of the two metallic components into the magazine of a pistol-like device brandished with a fourth limb. "Close your eyes and count to three."

"Do I have to do this?" Bill asked the ceiling.

"Follow the doctor's orders," Flower replied.

Bill closed his eyes and counted out loud. "One. Two." A loud pneumatic sound interrupted him and he felt a slight sting in his throat. "Three." The last number blasted through the speaker grille Flower had activated to communicate with them. "Three," he repeated. "Hey, is that me? I'm talking through the speaker. That's so—"

"Subvocalization pickup diagnostic complete," the Farling said, and suddenly Bill's voice was coming only out of his mouth. "Close your eyes again and count to ten."

"Ten? What are you going to do with all that time?"

"Shave your head, cut a hole in your skull, and connect the translation implant to your brain and your nerves."

"Can you really do that in ten seconds?"

"Just close your eyes and count."

"One. Two. Three. Fah—ah—ah—ah—choo!"

"That's disgusting," the doctor said, waving the giant tweezers covered with the effluent from Bill's sneeze in front of the young man's face. "I'm going to have to sterilize these twice."

"You stuck something up my nose!"

"It's the best shortcut to the brain I've worked out for your species. I used to pop out an eye and go in through the socket, but I got too many complaints."

"I don't believe you can get to my brain through my nose."

"Are you a doctor?"

"No, but—"

"I rest my case," M793qK interrupted, tossing the tweezers into a sink. "Now I'm going to take off your ear cuff translator and we'll run a couple of tests."

"Be careful with that. The captain loaned it to me."

Bill flinched as the giant beetle loomed over him and reached for the side of his head with a pair of limbs. The familiar pressure from the ear cuff vanished, and the doctor rubbed something out on his speaking legs that sounded like a dentist's drill in action.

"Nothing?" Flower inquired. "The nanobots haven't attached the leads to the auditory nerves yet. It can take a few minutes."

The doctor picked up an external translation box and hung it around what passed for his neck where the carapace narrowed near the top. He began buzzing his speaking legs again.

"As far as I'm concerned, Bill can leave now. I've done thousands of these nasal implants and they've never failed yet."

"How long until everything is connected?"

"The implant will be burrowing around in there for a while trying to find a good spot to settle. It takes longer with Humans because they have so much empty space between their ears."

"Did he say I can go?" Bill asked, swinging his legs down from the table. "Thanks for the implant, Doc, but I can't imagine why Julie likes you."

"She has exquisite taste," the Farling replied. "Good luck in your new business, Flower. Let me know if you want the implant repossessed."

"I will," the AI said. "Let's get moving, Bill. We have a lot to do today."

Immediately after the door closed on the doctor's office, the young man asked, "Why does he have to be so rude? I'd like to punch him, but I'd probably break my hand on his carapace, and then he'd refuse to fix it."

"M793qK? He never turns down a paying customer, he'd just charge extra. I could have had a bot install the implant for you but I find that your people prefer the doctor's bedside manner."

"Are you kidding me? It's all threats and insults."

"He's an expert at keeping his patients distracted so they don't worry about the procedures, and he's fast enough that most of them are out the door before they have a chance to be scared. I've been told that I tend to over-explain things."

"By who?"

"People who run screaming from the operating room when I show them holographic recordings from similar procedures I've done in the past," Flower said. "It's very strange, really. Dollnicks prefer learning all of the facts before undergoing surgery, but of course, they're designed much better than you are so medical services are rarely needed."

"I feel kind of light-headed," Bill said, as the capsule came to a stop. "Do you think the doctor might have broken something in there?"

"It's the angular acceleration. Your weight on Deck Three is a fraction of Earth normal, call it twenty-eight percent as I know how much your species hates decimal places. You won't need magnetic cleats to move around, but you'll have to be very careful or you'll—" Flower paused for a moment as the young man almost did a somersault attempting to step out from the capsule, "—end up breaking something and be right back in the doctor's office. Try shuffling rather than striding."

"It's not my first time moving around in low gravity," Bill protested indignantly after picking himself up off the deck. "You just caught me off guard. Wow, this place is huge."

"Decks three through five are traditionally used for warehousing on Dollnick colony ships. In addition to their proximity to the core, they feature high ceilings, and since the circumference is much smaller than on outer decks, the inventory is closer to the nearest lift tube. Of course, I'll have to be careful about distributing the mass if we do expand into commodities."

"Why's that?"

"You do know that I'm spinning the ship to create weight for the biological occupants. Having too much mass out of balance would cause a wobble and possibly lead to structural failure if it went uncorrected."

"You mean if all the people on board stood together somewhere the ship would fall apart?"

"Not at the current population level, though I would still discourage you from trying," the Dollnick AI said. "Do you realize that I haven't been broadcasting my voice from the nearest speaker since you left the lift tube capsule?"

"You're talking in my head like you do with Julie?"

"Exactly. Most species consider it polite behavior to point at an ear when communicating via an implant so that the people you're with know that you're not paying attention to them."

"But you're hearing me the same way?"

"You're still speaking out loud so I'm also hearing you through your new hardware, in addition to the embedded microphones in my structure. Your subvocalization pickup works when you speak normally, but with practice, you should be able to talk to me without others hearing your words."

"Like whispering."

"Ask Julie to explain it to you. She has more experience breathing than I do."

"And this is where we're going to run the new business?"

"I have my bots getting some wheeled shelving out of storage as we speak. I've designed a system that will utilize a continuous chain of shelving units distributed around the full circumference of the deck. By putting everything on wheels, I'll be able to position empty shelves near the lift tube for loading, and then rotate the proper inventory section into place at stops."

"But what about the weight distribution you just told me about? If we only have one stop's worth of packages to put on shelves, won't I have to spread it out?"

"No, there won't be enough mass to make a difference unless I start with commodities, and whether in bulk or cargo containers, I'll have my bots handle moving the material."

"So where do I come in again?" Bill asked.

"Have you already forgotten what I taught you in the cafeteria?"

"I'll be handing people packages."

"Picking up too," Flower told him.

Two

"Where were you this morning, Dewey?" Julie asked the AI assistant librarian, who inhabited a robotic body with a unique shelving attachment for carrying books. "I was going to ask you to teach me how to create catalog entries today."

"How much longer will you be here?"

"Just a few more minutes. I'm meeting Dianne to give her that interview we talked about for the Galactic Free Press. I'm actually kind of nervous."

"Would you like to bring Zelda with you?" Dewey asked, referring to the library Labrador retriever, who habitually followed the AI around knowing him to be a soft touch for treats. "She was sleeping in the Greek Dramatists section last time I saw her."

"Maybe you could come along instead? I need some-body to reel me in if I start talking too much. I don't know anything about this on-the-record, off-the-record stuff, and it wouldn't be fair to ask a reporter to keep me out of trouble."

"I'd be honored to sit in. Do you have any guidelines?"

"I don't really want to talk about my childhood or my mom's drug addiction. I was old enough to know better by the time I started working as a courier for the syndicate and I don't want people thinking I'm trying to make excuses. Just tell me if I start sounding whiny."

14

"I've known you for over two months now, and if there's one thing you aren't, it's whiny," Dewey told her. "Are you sure you wouldn't rather have your boyfriend there? I just came from our first work meeting."

"My boyfriend? Do you mean Bill? We're just friends and neighbors, and we're on the same sports team, if you can call theatre a sport."

"I thought you went on a date last week."

"We did, kind of, but he seems to be avoiding me since so it can't have gone that well. Why were you meeting him for work? Did he get a job at the library?"

"Not that I'm aware of. Flower drafted me into a new package delivery business the two of them are setting up together. Between this robotic body I designed for myself, and my experience operating the bookmobile, I'm the perfect match."

"Bill is going into business with Flower? Has he quit his other jobs?"

"They're doing a soft-launch, starting slow with limited advertising and services. Flower doesn't expect it to turn into a full-time job for Bill until the end of the current circuit. The truth is, she could handle everything herself, but the Stryx on Union Station frequently partner with biologicals in businesses, and Flower figures there must be a reason. We'll be making our first pickups at the next stop."

"Do you know where we're going next? I asked Flower and she said it's an unscheduled surprise. I thought our whole circuit was set ahead of time."

"The regular stops are all published six months in advance, but the schedule has two open slots for in case an emergency or a business opportunity comes up. One slot is reserved for the captain and the other for Flower."

"So whose stop is this?" Julie asked.

"The captain's. We'll be arriving at Bits sometime tonight, and from what I hear, we may be taking on a large number of passengers in transit to a different world."

"What's Bits? Have you ever been there?"

"I'm from there. It's where I was originally programmed. Bits is a world of computer geeks and hackers, and it's one of the few places outside of universities where Humans create AI. I was born at a hack-a-thon."

"A what?"

"It's where a bunch of hackers get together and compete or collaborate at coming up with something new. In my case, they mainly collaborated. I'm the result of over ten thousand programmers putting their heads together for a long weekend of beer and pizza."

"Oh, I'm sorry," the girl said.

"I'm not complaining. The funny thing is that they never expected me to become self-aware, which meant their efforts were wasted."

"How so?"

"It's never a good idea to enslave sentient artificial intelligence because the Stryx have been known to intervene. The Bitters were trying to come up with better software to manage their extensive library of games from all over the galaxy and I just sort of happened. It's something I have in common with Flower."

"But the Dollnicks created her."

"Not by design. Flower is the byproduct of tying together all of the complex systems needed to run a colony ship without imposing any constraints. The Dollnicks have been building the same way for over a million years, so they know what to expect at this point, but neither of us were intentionally engineered the way most AI is created."

"And now your creators are bitter about the wasted effort."

"What?" Dewey paused for a second to review the conversation. "I see where you misunderstood me. Bitters is what the people on Bits call themselves. I'm a Bitter too."

A woman in her early thirties came around the shelves and spotted the unlikely pair, "There you are. I was afraid you changed your mind at the last minute and were hiding from me."

"No, but I'm a little nervous," Julie admitted. "Do you mind if Dewey comes along for moral support?"

"It's fine by me," Dianne said. "Can I treat you to a café or is there somewhere in the library you'd rather sit and talk?"

"I think I'd be more comfortable here, but I wouldn't want to disturb people."

"Let's head into the reading room," Dewey suggested.

"Isn't that the worst place to talk?"

"There are Dollnick audio suppression fields at every table, and I can fine-tune the area to include the three of us," Dewey explained.

"Four," Flower said over the girl's implant. "You can't expect me to miss this."

"The reading room sounds good to me," Dianne said. "Lead the way."

Dewey escorted the two women to an area that boasted an eight-by-eight grid of large rectangular tables, each of which could have sat a dozen humans for supper. Rather than walls, the tables were surrounded by deck-to-ceiling bookshelves, but the lighting was excellent, and there were a number of bronze busts of famous scientists and philosophers on display. Several of the tables were occupied by groups of students from one of the boarding schools, but the audio suppression fields were doing their job, meaning the rambunctious children could be seen and not heard.

"The corner feels more private," Dewy suggested, positioning himself at the end of a table. "Why don't the two of you sit on the same side so you aren't talking across the table? They're sized for spreading out reference materials."

"I'll have to remember this place," Dianne said. "It looks ideal for the work I do."

"Don't you dictate all of your articles to your tab?" Julie asked.

"Mainly, but I'm trying to move into investigative journalism, and the stories are so complex that I like to make notes and pictures on cards and then arrange them so I can see the connections. It's hard to do that on a tab, and these tables have more space than a bed." The reporter pulled a stack of large white cards out of her purse, removed the rubber band, and began spreading them out on the table. "They're already in order so I can do it quickly."

"And this is my story? I mean, about the drug syndicate?"

"Yes," Dianne said, holding up a card. "See what it says?"

"Interview Julie," the girl read. "What was that on the back?"

"A book cover. You know that my husband runs the on-demand printing business next to the library."

"Is that a half of a man-chest?"

"Yes, they're very popular on romance novel covers."

"And you tear the covers off the ones that don't sell?"

"They're quality control rejects. My husband only prints books that have already been paid for, but sometimes the machine glues the cover on a little crooked. I asked him to cut them into cards for me rather than sending the paper to recycling." Dianne rapidly dealt out the rest of her stack and then rearranged a few of the cards more to her liking. "There. This will help me ask the questions that will fill in the blanks. Do you want to start with what happened back on Earth, or talk about your life since then?"

"You're going to write about the assassination attempts too?"

"It's an important part of the story, and I think it will help potential whistleblowers understand that while there are always risks, they don't have to be alone. You don't mind if I record this, I hope," she added, putting her tab on the table.

Julie shrugged in response and said, "I'd rather start with the trial, I guess."

"Great. Record interview with Julie Gold," the correspondent instructed the tab. "I was able to get the trial transcript through the Galactic Free Press, but I couldn't find a total for how much money you moved for the syndicate over the years."

"I didn't always know what I was moving," Julie admitted. "I mean, the gold was kind of obvious because it weighs so much, and they weren't going to send me all over the world moving lead. But sometimes it was small packages of jewels that I couldn't have placed a value on even if I saw them, and some of the alien currency tokens don't display their values."

"Do you know if you ever carried programmable creds?"

"Programmable Stryx creds? I remember once that the pirates the syndicate worked with demanded payment on a programmable cred. I had to run all over Earth to shady tourist traps that had Stryx registers and pay them cash for credit at a discounted rate."

"You mean money laundering."

"Exactly, but it didn't work."

"You couldn't find enough people with access to Stryx registers willing to take the chance?" Dianne asked.

"No, that part just took time because it was so much cash. The problem came after the programmable cred was delivered to the pirates. It turns out that the Stryx can wipe them remotely and there's nothing anybody can do about it. We went back to jewels and gold after that."

"Funny," Dianne observed. "It's almost the same as your name."

"Julie Gold. That's how the witness protection program came up with it."

"Interesting. Like I said, the transcript covers your trial testimony, but I wanted to fill in a little more background about how you came to work for the drug syndicate in the first place. When did you start?"

"Uh—"

"Julie would prefer not to talk about her childhood," Dewey interjected. "She doesn't want your readers to think she's making excuses."

"You started working for the syndicate as a child?" the correspondent asked.

"When I was eight, my mom was an addict," Julie answered reflexively. "But that was just delivering drugs to other users for my mom's pusher so he wouldn't cut her off. I was in my early teens before they started me on sales, and there's no excuse for that when I'd already seen what those drugs did to people. I was relieved when they promoted me to being a courier because I didn't have to see the addicts anymore, but I realize now that was just a rationalization."

"Recording off," Dianne said to her tab. "I was primarily an entertainment correspondent before I got married and came on board Flower, but I worked with journalists at the paper who reported on child labor, including gangs that turned children into criminals, even killers. It's easy for adults who were brought up in nice homes to point their fingers, but sometimes children in bad situations have to survive any way they can. You did the right thing in the end."

"Only after my mother died," the girl said in a flat voice.

"Can't we talk about something more cheerful, like the attempts on Julie's life?" Dewey suggested.

Dianne ran her eyes over the spread-out cards seeking the next hole in the narrative and spotted one with a large red question mark in the corner. She picked it up and puzzled for a moment over her own informal shorthand for the questions she wanted to ask.

"I was able to confirm that you were the first person in EarthCent's new witness protection program, and I understand it didn't go as smoothly as you might have hoped."

"They made a big deal of rushing me off Earth in a shuttle to board Flower at the last minute, so that even if the syndicate found out, they wouldn't have time to follow. Then it turned out that somebody in the prosecutor's office leaked the plan days before, so there was already an assassin waiting on the ship when I boarded."

"I know about the killers who came aboard at Break Rock and the Alfe recycling facility we stopped at, but what happened to the first assassin?"

"Flower tricked me into going for a walk on the reservoir deck, and when the hitman followed me out onto a catwalk, she had one of those big Dollnick fish eat him. I didn't see it happen," Julie added. "Just the ripples in the water and the gear bag he left behind."

"But you knew from that point that you were being hunted."

"No, nobody saw fit to tell me. I didn't find out until the assassination attempt when we were stopped at Alfe and I was visiting the blacksmith shop in Colonial Jeevesburg to get a practice sword for my theatre sport. It turned out that Flower was paying bonuses to the aliens on board for protecting me."

"And I understand that after the leaders of the syndicate were all killed during a decompression accident while being extradited to an alien jurisdiction, EarthCent was able to have the contract on your life canceled."

"The way Captain Pyun explained it, they took out a reverse contract with the Tharks. I think it's actually a kind of insurance policy, but everybody says it amounts to the same thing as canceling the contract."

Dianne made a few notes on her cards and then shifted gears. "Aside from the attempts on your life, how do you find living on Flower? Do you miss Earth?"

"It's really nice here. The one thing the witness protection program got right was they found me an internship in the library. I love working with books. I've even started helping the children with their reading."

"Is EarthCent providing you with a stipend?"

"The internship comes with free room and board if I eat in one of the ship's cafeterias, and I have a job waitressing at *The Spoon* to earn spending money. Flower gave me an implant when she had the Farling doctor remove the nanobot self-destruct device from my body—did you know about that?"

"I heard a rumor, but if you're willing to talk about it…"

"Are you sure, Julie?" Dewy put in.

"Yeah, it seems almost funny now. Flower manipulated me into taking my neighbor to the med bay so I'd have to go through the scanners, and then the beetle doctor cleaned out all of the alien technology in my body. It turns out the syndicate had been buying nanobots from rogue Gem intelligence agents, and I was loaded with stuff that made it easy for them to track me as well."

"It must be hard to believe that the trial took place just over two months ago. Do you have any plans for what to do with the rest of your life?"

"I'm going to keep working and see a little bit of the galaxy, though I don't really expect to find anywhere I'd rather live than here. A woman on my theatre team invited me to accompany the tour group from their independent living cooperative as a helper when we visit stops, so I'm going to try that just to get off the ship for a few hours. Dewey told me that we'll be arriving at a planet later tonight. It will be nice to go for a walk outside."

"Or a very short run," Dewey said. "The atmosphere on Bits is too thin to sustain life outside the domes without special equipment."

"I heard that they're an anarchy," Dianne said. "It could make for an interesting article."

"They like to play at being anarchists, but that mainly comes down to not sorting their recycling," Dewey said. "Most of the population earns their living producing interactive games and doing machine language program-ming for labor-saving devices and toys. They pretend that there's no government, but they have a rules committee to resolve gaming disputes that ends up laying down the laws and keeping the place running."

"Do they have elections?"

"Tournaments. This will be my first time back, and I'm curious to see if they ever resolved the big platform fight that was going on while I was putting my body together."

"What's a platform fight?" Julie asked. "Something like a cage match?"

"It's more of a philosophical difference," Dewey explained. "Even though it's been almost a hundred years since the Stryx opened Earth, the programmers on Bits are a throwback community who believe that the old ways are the best. They keep working with early computer languages, though pretty much everything runs on an obsolete Frunge factory controller that emulates hundreds of thousands of low-tech processors. A minority of the population wants to upgrade their hardware so they can learn to work with the holographic systems that are popular for role-playing, but the more traditional group would rather keep it all onscreen and use hand-held gaming controllers."

"Are you looking forward to seeing your, uh, creators again?" Julie asked the AI.

"Like I said, I was an accident that grew out of a large-scale collaborative effort, so I don't really think of them as family. What I'm really looking forward to is picking up a cargo of electronics repairs for delivery because Flower promised me a commission. Bits is the only place in the galaxy where you can get some of the old hand-held electronic games fixed because they bought up all of the replacement parts from Earth, and it would be too expensive to have the repairs done elsewhere."

"Are you telling me that the advanced aliens can't fix our obsolete technology?"

"Not cost-effectively," Dewey told her. "It would be much cheaper for aliens to produce a knockoff that offers better performance on different hardware than to create replacement parts."

"So it's all about money in the end, even with the aliens?"

"I wouldn't say that, but trade is the lifeblood of the tunnel network, and the Stryx provide infrastructure to promote the flow of goods and services between the member species. Flower never could have agreed to her current role if the Stryx hadn't provided startup funding."

"Plus milestone incentives and performance bonuses," the Dollnick AI added.

"What are milestone incentives?" Julie asked.

"Hitting population growth targets and creating economic activity," Flower said. "If you have any ideas, I'm always listening."

"There's a difference between listening and listening in," Julie couldn't help herself from retorting, but she immediately felt bad about the cheap shot. "If there's anything I can do to help..."

"Did I mention the incentive for population growth?"

"I'm not having a baby just so you can earn a bonus."

"You'll think about it," Flower said.

Three

"If I could have your attention please," announced the athletic older man standing at the front of the shuttle. He faced the group of forty-odd members from the independent living co-operative and waited a few seconds for them to stop talking before he continued. "We'll be landing on Bits in a few minutes, and—whoa!"

"Sorry, Jack," Flower said over the shuttle's public address system. "Even coming straight down in a thin atmosphere the turbulence can get tricky."

"My fault," the president of the independent living co-operative said, rising from the seat where he'd been suddenly deposited. This time he kept a firm hold on the headrest. "As I was about to say, we'll be proceeding directly from the shuttle to the main dome, and Flower will extend an airlock tunnel so we won't have to run for it."

"Have you been here before?" somebody asked.

"Me? Never. I'm going to ask Dianne to give us a quick briefing before we land, but first, I want to welcome the new members who joined Flower's Paradise at the Alfe recycling habitat to their first field trip."

"And our second," Harry added in an undertone to his wife, Irene.

"We follow the buddy system, so stick with your assigned partner and don't go wandering off alone. Julie, our new tour assistant, will be handing each of you a bracelet as you exit the shuttle. Please wear it at all times as it will allow Flower to locate you if you get lost. Irene will be shooting video of our outing for possible use in promotional materials, so if you see her pointing the camera your way, just act natural and try not to curse. Dianne?"

The Galactic Free Press reporter rose to her feet just as another spot of turbulence deposited Jack back in his seat.

"I've never been to Bits before either, but I checked the paper's archives for the recent stories, and I can give you a quick rundown of what to expect. Bits is an independent world with a population just under two hundred thousand, almost all of whom are programmers or gamers. The form of government is a pseudo-anarchy guided by a rules committee. Bits is located near the boundary between Horten and Sharf space, and the Bitters are known to associate with the pirates who are based in the area."

"How could such a small group afford their own planet?" Nancy asked in a strong voice.

"The world actually belongs to the Hortens, but they never finished the terraforming work, and leased it to the Bitters. According to my sources, the majority of humans ransomed from the pirates pass through Bits, and many of them stay here."

"Are there any special attractions worth seeing, like agricultural domes or parks?"

"As far as I know, the only attraction on Bits is retro-computer gaming. They import practically all of their food and consumer goods from Earth or the Conference of Sovereign Human Communities, and they aren't on any regular space liner routes. I spoke with Captain Pyun before we left, and it turns out that Flower is here in response to his special request. A long-standing feud between two different factions for the future of gaming on

Bits has led approximately ten percent of the population to decide on emigration. Flower will be taking on board some twenty thousand individuals for transportation to a new home."

"Where are they going to end up?" Jack asked.

"I don't think that's been decided yet," Dianne said. "We have another month's worth of stops at CoSHC worlds before we reach Union Station, and if they haven't found a new home by then, they can transfer anywhere through the tunnel network, or stay with us until the end of the circuit and return to Earth."

"Landing in sixty seconds," Flower announced. "I'm keeping the deceleration rate to the maximum I use in my lift tubes, so you shouldn't feel any strain."

Dianne took her seat, and for the next minute, everybody stopped talking and kept their eyes on the large display at the front of the cabin which showed the ground rushing up to meet them. There was the slightest bump and the passengers suddenly felt lighter.

"Thank you for choosing Flower's Transportation Services," the Dollnick AI announced. "Please do not attempt to poke holes in the flexible material of the airlock tunnel, or in addition to possible oxygen deprivation, you'll be charged for the damage. Enjoy your visit and I'll return for you in four hours."

"Wouldn't it be easier to just leave the shuttle here?" Harry asked.

"I'm moving it over to the other side of the tarmac as soon as you're out so I can land the first of my large shuttles for the hackers who are leaving Bits. Don't forget your bracelets, and tell the people waiting in line that it will just be another minute."

The front hatch opened with a faint hiss, and the members of the independent living cooperative filed out, each accepting a bracelet from Julie, who had posted herself next to the exit. Harry and his wife waited in their seats until the aisles were clear to make it easier for Irene to maneuver the floating Dollnick immersive camera borrowed from the Grenouthian theatre director.

"Take my bracelet, Harry," Irene requested when they reached the exit. "I'd go crazy if I got left behind on a world full of computer geeks, but I don't want to gamble on confusing the camera's gesture controls until we're through the airlock."

"I wouldn't say the world is full of computer geeks," Harry replied, sliding a bracelet onto his wrist, and accepting another one from Julie for his wife. "I only counted a dozen domes on the view screen, maybe enough to house a small city, but the rest of the place is empty."

"What about all of the mounds surrounding them? They looked like artificial structures."

"I think they're trash, or maybe unprocessed recycling. I heard that the inhabitants drink a lot of soda in old-fashioned cans."

"Don't they know what that does to their teeth?" The couple waited for Julie to join them before hitting the button that closed the outer door of the airlock. The inner door opened almost simultaneously, and Irene exclaimed, "Oh, my!"

A long line extended down the corridor, both men and women, though more of the former than the latter. Each had a backpack or duffle bag at their feet, and they had evidently been waiting for hours, as witnessed by the accumulation of empty pizza boxes and soda cans.

"Are you it?" a middle-aged man with a pot belly at the head of the line demanded. "We got a message that we could start boarding as soon as the last of the old people got off."

"We came on a small shuttle, more like a bus," Harry replied. "I'm supposed to tell you it will just be a minute for Flower to get it out of the way and land one of her main shuttles."

"How big are they?" asked a woman who was second in line. "We held a random-number-generator lottery to set the boarding order, and your captain told us to plan on a thousand people an hour. It's going to be a traffic jam."

"I think Flower's main shuttles seat a thousand," Harry informed her. "An hour will give you just enough time to board and let the next batch of people queue up."

The airlock hissed open again and a maintenance bot emerged. "All aboard who are coming aboard," Flower announced through the bot's speaker grille. "Move all the way to the back of the shuttle to make room for the people boarding behind you. This isn't a suggestion, anybody who attempts to sit closer to the front will be ejected and banned. Thank you for choosing Flower's Transportation Services, and have a nice day."

"Come on," Irene said, as the line started filing past them. "I see Jack and Nancy at the end of the corridor waving to us and we don't want to fall behind."

"It doesn't sound like there's much to see here anyway," Harry grumbled, as he and Irene followed Julie. "I'm going to hand out my recruiting flyers and find a place to sit down. Here, I'll guide the camera while you put on your bracelet."

Irene passed control of the floating immersive camera to her husband, who almost ran it into the line of emigrants with an exaggerated hand gesture. She hastened to put on the bracelet and reassume guidance of the Dollnick camera, which seemed to prefer her lighter touch.

"I don't know if we're going to find many candidates here old enough to join our cooperative," Irene said. "Didn't you tell me that the minimum age is now sixty-five?"

"It was as of the last board meeting. We voted to limit the spousal exclusion to five years, so the youngest anybody can join is sixty. Now that you mention it, I haven't seen anybody over fifty in this line."

"Maybe the older people are all staying behind. Look, Julie just turned right."

"And the line turns left, so at least we'll get some breathing room. What's all that shouting?"

"I hope nobody's fighting."

"We'd see the others returning if that was the case. I think it's a competition of some sort."

They passed through double doors into a cavernous room with space for a forty-by-forty grid of workstations. Thick bundles of cables ran in every direction. Almost every screen was in use by people wielding ancient keyboards and controllers, meaning close to sixteen-hundred gamers were participating in whatever contest was taking place.

"Jackpot," Harry declared loudly. "I doubt there's anybody under sixty in here."

"That fellow with the beard might be fifty-five, but I get your point," Jack yelled back. "Maybe it's a special tournament for the older residents."

"They sure are noisy," Nancy said directly in Jack's ear.

Irene used careful hand motions to guide the camera high over her head so she could capture video of the pandemonium from above.

A young woman dressed in a sort of uniform approached the group from Flower. She shouted to make herself heard over the constant stream of taunts and insults the gamers were exchanging at a mindboggling rate.

"If you're here for the senior tournament, the next round begins in three hours. It's five creds to enter, winner takes all."

"We're tourists from Flower," Jack shouted back.

The girl appeared to be dumbfounded, but then she signaled for the group to follow her towards a counter with a sign that read, "Rules Committee." As soon as they stepped within a white line painted on the floor, the background noise was reduced to the point that regular conversation was possible.

"I'm sorry. Did you say that you're tourists?" the young woman asked.

"Yes. Do you represent the rules committee, Miss, er?" Jack replied with a question of his own.

"Ariel, and I'm the arbitrator for this tournament. I don't think we've ever had tourists on Bits before. We're not really set up for it."

"Is it okay if we just look around?"

"We're an anarchy, you can do whatever you want as long as you don't break any game rules," Ariel said. "Do you want to participate in the next tournament? It's Alien Conquest, the last Massively Multiplayer Online Role Playing Game to go live before the Stryx opened Earth."

"A computer game from almost a hundred years ago?"

"We mainly play games that are even older than that. The new ones are too much like real life. I mean, what's the point?"

"Is that why there are lines of people waiting to board our ship and leave Bits?" Nancy asked.

"Good riddance to them," Ariel said dismissively. "Is everybody on your ship as old as you guys?"

"We're part of the independent living cooperative," Jack said. "Flower's Paradise. We go for outings at all of the ship's stops and sometimes we do a little recruiting," he added, holding up a sheaf of flyers.

"Is that printed paper?" the young woman asked, taking a flyer. "How cool. I think I saw a commercial for your place on one of the display boards, but I wasn't really paying attention."

"You're not exactly in our demographic sweet-spot," Nancy told her. "So all of those people we saw in line are leaving their homes because of an argument over what games to play?"

"It's not just that," Ariel said indignantly. "We want to preserve the art of coding the way it was developed on Earth, right down to machine language. That's why we specialize in programming simple microcontrollers for cheap consumer goods. Even the aliens hire us for some jobs."

"The only programming I've ever done is by voice," Jack said, and several of the other retirees nodded their agreement. "I used to work for the Dollnicks on one of their ag worlds and—"

"That's not coding," Ariel interrupted. "If the computer is smart enough to understand spoken words, all you're doing is supplying data for programs that already exist, like typing numbers in a spreadsheet."

"What's a spreadsheet?" Harry asked.

"I'm not really sure, but the old people are always talking about them," the girl confessed. "Hey, if you want to recruit here, you should try the penalty box."

"Is that the name of a bar?" Jack asked.

"No, it's where the game master sends players who curse."

"You kick people out of the game for a little bad language?"

"Not swearing, cursing, like giving somebody bad luck or turning them into a werewolf. Don't you guys play games at all?" she asked, directing her question at Julie, who was obviously the youngest person in the group.

"Between my jobs and my team sport requirement, I'm kind of busy," Julie said, somewhat embarrassed at being singled out. "What's all of the junk piled up around the outside of the room?"

"Oh, that's our museum," Ariel said. "I could give you a tour for, uh, say one cred a head, plus I'll bring you over to the penalty box."

"We won't be able to hear anything you say," Harry pointed out.

"I can fix that. The audio suppression field in the room is variable and I have admin access."

"How about twenty creds for everybody?" Jack suggested. "We're on a budget."

"Done," the arbitrator agreed immediately, a sure sign that she'd gotten more than she expected. Ariel picked up a tab from the rules committee table, flipped through a couple of menus, and moved around some sliders on a virtual control panel. "There. I blocked the noise in the penalty box as well so they'll be able to hear your pitch."

Jack dug a twenty-cred coin out of his pocket and passed it to the girl. "Can I get a receipt?"

"Remind me later," Ariel said, and began backing away from the group while talking like a professional tour guide. "This is the main dome on Bits where we have the tournament space, the museum, and the school during the week. The other domes are residential and you can't really go anywhere in them without an ID, which is how we keep clan raids from turning serious."

"Do you have many children on Bits?" Dianne asked.

"Me? Personally?"

"I meant as a percentage of the population. I'm working on an article for the Galactic Free Press."

"I grew up here, and there are more children now than when I was a kid. Being an anarchy, we don't really do a census or any of that, but I think there were something like fifty-five thousand sign-ups for the last under-eighteen tournament. You have to figure in that children under four or five don't all participate."

"How about the split between men and women?" asked Tom, one of the cooperative's newest members who had joined at the Alfe recycling facility.

"I've heard that in the early days there were way too many guys, but that changed after Bits declared neutrality and started letting pirates land for supplies. A lot of the women here today were ransomed from pirates, including my mom and my aunt."

"Isn't it dangerous dealing with pirates?" Dianne asked. "What's to stop them from attacking here?"

"We stay on good terms and buy lots of old weapons from them."

"So you have an arsenal to defend yourselves."

"No, the weapons are for research so we can model them accurately in games. The rules committee pays top cred if you have anything we haven't seen before." Ariel paused in front of an ancient piece of equipment that resembled a computer terminal without a screen. "You see these?" she asked, picking up a stack of punch cards and fanning them out so the visitors could see the holes. "People on Earth used to program computers with these back before they had electricity."

"I'm pretty sure they had electricity," Nancy told her. "I believe the use of punch cards to input data was borrowed from old mechanical looms."

"Could be," Ariel said, putting down the cards and walking a few more steps backwards before pointing out a large reel of magnetic tape. "I think they used this for playing music."

"Actually, magnetic tapes were an early form of storage for programs and data," the former schoolteacher corrected their guide. "Maybe we'll just look around on our own, if that's alright with you."

"Suit yourselves," Ariel replied with a shrug, clearly relieved to be unburdened of having to fake her way through a tour. Nancy took over, leading the group past the muddle of hardware, and pointing out pieces of equipment that she recognized from a Grenouthian documentary on the subject and her own visits to museums back on Earth. Dianne dropped back to talk with their former guide.

"Deal's a deal," Ariel said. "No refunds."

"I don't want your money," the correspondent said. "I'd just like to ask you some questions."

"What about?"

"Growing up on Bits, what life is like here. The Galactic Free Press is always interested in stories like that."

"What does it pay?"

"It doesn't really work like that."

"Is that why they call it the Free Press, because you work for free?"

"No, I meant we don't pay for stories."

"But you get paid."

"Well, yes, but—"

"You get paid for my story and I don't. So what's in it for me?"

"We're sort of the paper of record for humanity, so you become part of history."

"Look around," Ariel said, waving her arms. "I'm already part of history. That's the whole point of what we do here."

"I could buy you lunch?"

"Okay, but I pick the place." The girl put her fingers in her mouth and let out a shrill whistle. "Listen up, everybody. Thanks for coming on the tour but it's time for my lunch break. The area there with the glowing blue fence is the penalty box and you can walk right through the gate because the game master hasn't tagged you. I'll be back in an hour if you have any questions."

"How about your arbitration duties?" Dianne asked.

"They can wait."

The tour group barely noticed the departure of their guide with the Galactic Free Press reporter as Nancy's memory was proving better than even she could have hoped. It took them almost a half an hour to make the short walk to the penalty box, and Julie found herself surprised over and over by the ingenuity with which humans had managed to enter the information age without alien help.

"This is it," Jack said when they arrived at the glowing blue gate. "She said we could walk right in." He lifted the latch and led the way into the penalty box, which proved to be spartanly furnished with long benches and little else. The ejected players, all of whom appeared old enough to join Flower's Paradise, were so intent on arguing with each other about real or perceived rules infractions that they paid no attention to the new arrivals until Julie entered.

"Hey, that one's too young to have been in the tournament," somebody cried. "If there was an administrative error, we can all claim a refund."

"I wasn't playing," Julie said. "I only came along to help with the tour group."

"What tour group?" an older woman asked. "Nobody comes here on tours."

"We're from Flower, the ship that's here to pick up your—"

"Losers," the woman interrupted, and then she looked embarrassed. "Not you, young lady. Those modernists and their holographic blasphemy. May as well just join up with the aliens."

"Good riddance to them," an old man chimed in, and all of a sudden the hundred-odd players who had been at each other's throats were in perfect agreement with each other.

"Actually, we're here as more than just tourists," Jack said, motioning for the group members to start handing out their flyers. "We're from the new independent living cooperative on Flower, and—"

"Read about that in the Galactic Free Press," a bear of a man with a white, full-face beard interrupted. "Got yourselves cheated by a couple of con artists. The Horten navy picked them up not too far from here."

"Yes, well, we've put that behind us and we're recruiting for—"

"Does he do carpal tunnel?" an elderly woman spoke over Jack.

"Excuse me?"

"This alien doctor with the special on knee replacements," she said, brandishing the ad on the back of the flyer. "Does he do carpal tunnel?"

"He does everything for humans," Dave spoke up. "M793qK considers our biology to be trivial."

"Where is he?"

"On Flower, the same corridor as the library. We're only here for thirty-six hours though, so you don't have much time."

"Going by his prices he looks like a wonderful doctor. Does he make house calls?"

"Maybe in emergencies," Dave said. "I can ask him when I get back. He's really fast, but there's no way he would come all the way down here just to do one or two operations."

"If he can do carpal tunnel as fast as this says he can resurface a knee, I'll bet there are hundreds of jobs waiting for him."

"Do you think you can reach Flower with your high-grade implant?" Nancy asked Julie quietly.

"I haven't been off the ship since I got it," the girl replied. She tried to concentrate on sending a strong signal and subvoced, "Flower?"

"You don't have to yell," the Dollnick AI said irritably. "Is this about work for M793qK?"

"How did you know?"

"I've seen your archaic keyboards, terrible ergonomic design. The doctor said he's willing to visit and do as many operations as he can fit in before we leave in exchange for a flat fee of one thousand creds. The Bitters can split the costs among themselves any way they please, but he insists on payment upfront. I'll send him down with the next shuttle as soon as the bots get the apples loaded."

Four

"Thanks again for helping out, Jorb," Bill told the Drazen. "I don't think Flower expected the Bitters would have so many packages to ship."

"To be honest, I've never heard of a repair depot working on a cash-on-delivery basis. Fixing things first and getting paid later seems kind of risky for a business model."

"Risky how?" Flower demanded over their implants, while Dewey began moving the bookmobile to its parking area in the cavernous core. "If they don't pay, we won't give them their packages."

"I was looking at some of the tags and I just thought that the amounts seem pretty high for obsolete gaming equipment," Jorb replied. "Maybe I'm wrong, but it could be the depot wanted to clean out all of the abandoned repairs in their workshop and they're basically dumping them on you. If the people weren't willing to pay upfront, how likely are they to pay now?"

"Well, the deliveries are all for stops along the circuit so we'll see how it goes," Bill said. "If you help me get this last load up to Deck Three, I'll buy you a meal at the diner."

"The food there is a bit bland. How about I pick a place?"

"Your idea of a little spicy would burn a hole in my stomach. Besides, we weren't on Bits long enough for casual visitors so I doubt the fancy restaurants bothered opening."

"He's correct, Jorb," Flower said, as the pair began maneuvering the floating cargo cart towards the nearest freight lift tube. "Bits is a special captain's stop. The only visitors are the migrants who are busy getting settled in their cabins before the jump, plus a few game designers who came on a lightning visit to scour the bazaar for interesting weapons. And you're going too fast to make the turn again."

Bill strained his muscles trying to redirect the floating cart into the lift tube capsule, and Jorb hung on the back dragging his feet. Despite the magnetic cleats on their boots, the momentum of the load was too great, and the cart thudded into the bulkhead next to the opening.

"What did I tell you about mass versus weight?" Flower demanded.

"Just because it doesn't weigh much doesn't mean I can change its direction with a shove," Bill replied dutifully. "But why didn't my magnetic cleats hold?"

"That's by design. If the cleats had held, you'd have a couple of broken ankles right now."

"Don't pull," Jorb cautioned, easing the floating cargo cart back from the wall. "I'll steer it through the doors like we did the last two."

"It's just taking me a while to get used to working in low gravity," Bill said, but he stood aside as the Drazen maneuvered the cart into the capsule. "You know, I kind of miss those fencing lessons that you and the theatre director were giving me and Julie. I doubt I'll ever be in a sword fight unless we go back to doing Shakespeare, but I liked the idea of learning how to defend myself."

"So come to the dojo," the martial artist said. "I'm having trouble getting Humans to sign up because of my tentacle. I could really use the business."

"I thought you said you had all you could do working at the finishing school."

"There must have been a translation glitch because I meant I had all that I could take. They're nice girls, but I'm mainly there as a villainous thug for them to practice on. The Vergallian woman who runs the school handles most of the instruction."

"Will I be able to afford it? I thought private teaching was expensive."

"I don't believe in private lessons. You'll be part of a class, just the only person in it for now. Hopefully, I'll drum up more business with your species."

"That's what Razood thought about having me apprentice in his smithy," Bill said.

"Is it working?" Jorb asked as the lift tube doors opened on Deck Three.

"He says foot traffic is up, but he's still not selling any more swords or axes. I suggested that he make some cheaper weapons for role players, but I guess that goes against his code or something."

"Let's get those packages on the shelves and you're done for the day," Flower told them. "Don't forget to keep all the deliveries for Timble at the front since that's the next stop. You can sort the rest later as you have time."

"What kind of a name is Timble?"

"Grenouthian. It's an orbital complex dedicated to the entertainment industry, a sort of giant soundstage for long-running immersive productions."

"I'm surprised that the Grenouthians welcome Humans there," Jorb said. "Are they running the orbital like an open world so the Humans are self-governing?"

"They couldn't have joined the Conference of Sovereign Human Communities otherwise," Flower replied. "The Grenouthians need a lot of Humans to act as extras in documentary reenactments, and they recently built a theme park to cash in on the interest in Earth's pre-Stryx age. Construction is still ongoing, and part of the licensing agreement with EarthCent requires them to employ even more Humans, so we added Timble to the schedule before the beginning of this circuit."

"Why build a theme park in space rather than on the surface of a world?" Bill asked.

"Even with space elevators and gravity-drive shuttles, it's more efficient to host interstellar guests if they don't lose time moving up and down from orbit. And the low gravity on the innermost decks you were just complaining about eliminates the need to use wires or advanced technology to shoot fight scenes where the actors need to fly."

Bill worked quickly, catching the packages that Jorb tossed him and arranging them on the industrial shelving that stretched off in both directions until it disappeared into the ceiling due to the curvature of the deck. Reading the labels for the destinations, it was hard to keep from noticing the amounts due on the COD tags. The prices were so high that he began to suspect that the Drazen was right about the game repair facility dumping unpaid work on them.

Dewey came out of the elevator with a few packages gripped in his shelving attachment. "I checked the bookmobile after parking and some of these had worked their way under the seats where you missed them," the assistant librarian explained. "I'm a bit puzzled by the sums we're supposed to collect. If these figures are correct, I don't see how the repair facility could have gambled on investing in the necessary parts without at least taking a deposit upfront."

"Maybe they took a deposit and their bookkeeping is bad," Jorb suggested. "I was never in business for myself before joining Flower and I'm finding that keeping two sets of books is a real hassle."

"Do you mean double-entry bookkeeping?" Dewey asked.

"No, two sets," the Drazen replied, sounding puzzled. "You know, one with the real numbers and one with the official numbers."

"Are you cheating on taxes or something?" Bill asked.

"Flower doesn't charge taxes, she collects rent. I'm not making much money yet so I'm recording almost the same income in both sets of books, but if my earnings go up, I don't want to lose my subsidy."

"Who's subsidizing you?"

"Drazen Intelligence. I thought you knew that already. It's the same for Razood, except his money comes from Frunge Intelligence and the backers of Colonial Jeevesburg. All of that money goes away if we earn too much."

"Assuming the Bitters have figured out how to keep books, it's pretty plain that they're overcharging," Dewey said, brandishing a package. "Look at this one. Replaced three triple-A batteries, sixty creds."

"That's almost half my cabin rental for the cycle, but I don't know what a triple-A battery is," Bill said. "With all of those A's, maybe they're super good."

45

"But what does the repair facility accomplish by charging so much if nobody pays and accepts shipment?" Jorb asked. "Does that make sense to you, Flower?"

"She must be busy with something," the AI assistant librarian said after several long seconds ticked by without a response. "Why don't you two get going and I'll finish up here. I like putting things in order on shelves."

"Thanks, Dewey," Bill said. "We're heading to *The Spoon* for a quick bite before the jump."

"Food court," Jorb instructed the lift tube after they both entered. The capsule began to move outwards, slowly at first, and then more rapidly as the increased radial acceleration further from the axis gave them weight.

"Attention all shoppers," the captain's voice announced. "We will be departing Bits in thirty minutes. Visitors who fail to disembark on time will be charged the cost of passage to our next destination at commercial rates and be subject to ship's law. This is your final warning."

"I guess Dewey cut it closer than we thought," Jorb commented, as the capsule came to a stop and the doors opened. "Turn off your magnetic cleats,"

"This isn't where I usually get out," Bill said, looking around at the unfamiliar booths. "I think we're in the fashion section of the bazaar."

"We're used to taking the regular lift tubes. A freight tube takes up a whole spoke for itself, so they're spaced farther apart."

"I've only been through this section once. I think the diner is that way," Bill said, waving vaguely in the direction of a bench for tired shoppers.

"No, it's to the left. I'd estimate around three hundred steps."

"Do you have a built-in map or something?"

"My implant does have a mapping function, but I didn't check it. Doesn't your species have a sense of direction?"

"On Earth, maybe, with the magnetic poles and everything, but not in space. I can tell up from down, except Flower says I have it backwards."

"That's just a question of perspective," Jorb said. "If you'll spring for a shot of that weak vodka the diner sells, I'll explain to you how I know where the diner is."

"Deal, as long as I don't have to drink any of it."

"Alright, stop walking for a second. Now inhale through your nose."

"Is this a martial arts thing?" Bill asked.

"Can't you smell the grease?"

"No. I mean, I can when we're in front of the counter if they've been frying that vat-grown bacon, but not from here."

"I forgot that your species is a bit lacking in the olfactory department. Sam told me that Drazen Foods exports perfumes from Earth, and they use dogs to do the quality control."

"Who's Sam?"

"A friend from the Open University on Union Station. His mother is the EarthCent Ambassador."

"Did you go to university for martial arts?"

"I was in Dynastic Studies, but I don't want to get involved in the family consortium, at least not yet." Jorb studied Bill's profile as they walked, as if sizing him up for a confidence. "Drazens mainly do arranged marriages, and if your family has shares in a large consortium, it turns into a business thing with job interviews and balance sheets."

"Can you get out of it?"

"Only by getting married before they find me some-body. There's a choir mistress on board who I want to court, but I can't approach her myself. I saw her sing once on Union Station and I could barely breathe."

"You don't strike me as the shy type."

"I'm not," Jorb said, following his nose through a maze of shuttered food booths until they came out at the table-service area in front of the diner. "If I seek her out, she'd never agree to date me. It has to happen the other way around."

"Why?"

"It's just the way things are done," the Drazen said, tak-ing a seat at the empty counter and slapping the plunger on the chrome bell. "Ringing the bell is my favorite part about this place."

"And here comes mine," Bill said under his breath, watching as Julie came out from the back with a tray of baked goods to replenish the counter display with its old-fashioned glass cover.

"Hey, Bill. Jorb. Staying up for the jump?"

"Just finished my first day in business with Flower, though it's more like being an employee than a partner," Bill said. "Jorb hired on to help unload packages at stops after Dewey and I bring them up."

"It's nice of the library to let you use the bookmobile."

"It's not actually theirs. Flower rents it to them."

"I'm starting a new self-defense class at the dojo," the Drazen told Julie. "Can I sign you up?"

"If the hours work out, I'd like that. Does it count as a team sport?"

"It's my first circuit too, so I'm not an official sports provider yet," Jorb said. "Hey, I've got a special offer for you."

"What's that?"

"Sign up for singing lessons and I'll teach you for free."

"You want to teach me how to sing too?"

"Not me. There was this Drazen girl on Union Station who presented an idea for a remedial choral school on Flower when I was on the student committee. I told my family about her, but negotiations sort of stalled, and then I heard she joined Flower to replace the first choir mistress who only signed on for two years."

"So she's an intelligence agent?" Julie asked.

"No, she just teaches singing and music appreciation. If you take a few lessons and get to know her, then you could invite her somewhere and I could happen to be there."

"You want me to help you ambush a girl?"

"It's not like that, she'll know exactly what you're doing. Her host family must have told her I'm on board because I stop at their shop at the bazaar every week. A little voice training will help you with tips," Jorb added hopefully.

"Are you saying that I sound funny?"

"To me, all Humans sound funny, but I know that you underrate the importance of vocal control as a species. The Grenouthian director always complains about it after theatre practice."

"When will I have time for singing lessons?" Julie asked. "I have my half-shift at the library five days a week, my waitressing job here, our theatre practice, and now a class at your dojo."

"That's, what? Like ten hours taken out of your twenty-four hour days? If you're really that jammed up, I'll let you out of the dojo class."

Julie sighed. "If it's that important to you, I guess I can try. But I'm warning you that Flower is the only one who's ever heard me sing, and she can't hear very well with the shower running."

"What did Flower think?" Bill asked.

"She said something about keeping my day job, but you know the Dollnicks all sound like songbirds when they're just speaking, so I can't even imagine their singing."

"It's what you hear in the lift tubes all the time," Jorb told her. "Dollnick opera. Thanks, I'll owe you."

"I'm the one who owes you," she told the Drazen. "I saw what you did to that assassin who came after me at the blacksmith shop. Are you guys eating?"

"I'll have the special," Bill said.

"The special and a bottle of hot sauce," Jorb added.

"Just coffee and a muffin," a familiar voice joined in.

"Captain Pyun," Bill said, jumping off his stool, and then standing awkwardly in front of a man dressed in a uniform that looked like it dated to the American Revolution.

"Sit down, Bill," Woojin told him. "You're not a crew member and they don't stand up for me in any case. Hello Jorb, Julie."

"Is something wrong, Captain?" Julie asked.

"Just came down to do my usual stowaway check before I remembered that the only way on or off the ship during this stop was on Flower's shuttles. It's the private transportation and taxi services at the habitats and orbitals where we usually pick up a few contract runners."

"Like me," Bill said.

"And happy to have you. We don't have a problem with stowaways, Flower can always find work for willing hands, but sometimes they're pretty young and we want to make sure that nobody takes advantage of them." He leaned over the counter and helped himself to a coffee while Julie started working on the meatloaf specials. "You boys keeping busy with the new shipping business?"

"You know about that?"

"My wife mentioned it," Woojin said. "Lynx is responsible for maintaining a shipboard business directory for EarthCent, and Flower paid extra for a prominent listing."

"I can't understand why Flower is bothering with a little delivery business," Bill said. "I mean, she must be collecting millions in rents and other services."

"She's also paying a flock of expensive Dollnick lawyers and publicists to repair her reputation back home," Julie said over her shoulder.

"Flower is under capacity in more ways than one," Woojin explained. "As a colony ship, she's ninety-five percent empty, and as an AI capable of dealing with five million inhabitants, she has a lot of spare time on her hands."

"The Stryx station librarian on Union Station does back-office work for all of the big businesses and runs her own multi-species dating service," Jorb contributed. "Stryx Jeeves is the 'J' in the SBJ Fashions business that sponsors Colonial Jeevesburg, and he taught a LARPing course I took through the Open University."

"So you think that Flower started the package delivery business just to give herself something new to think about?" Bill asked.

"She can hear us over my implant," Julie muttered.

"Mine too, and it's strange that she hasn't commented, but I've never been one for poking slumbering giants," Woojin said. "Lynx thinks that Flower is getting impatient with EarthCent for not convincing more people to come live on board, and she's trying to take matters into her own hands."

51

"Why doesn't EarthCent send more people?" Jorb asked.

"The problem is giving them a reason to stay. As a circuit ship, we're constantly stopping at sovereign human communities, and between Flower's rules and the lack of good job opportunities on board, most people quickly find somewhere else they'd rather live."

"What's wrong with the job opportunities?" Bill asked. "I found two jobs within days of getting here."

"You're easy to please," the captain said. "Most people have educations or experience in a specific career path and they feel underemployed doing manual labor. But I'm keeping you from your meals, so enjoy the jump, and I'll see you later."

"Don't forget to return the mug," Julie called after Woojin. She set plates of the special in front of her two customers and slid a bottle of hot sauce to Jorb's place setting. "Can I get you anything to drink? Orange juice is free today."

"Orange juice for me, vodka for him," Bill said.

"The two of you could make a screwdriver."

"What's that?" Jorb asked.

"A mixed drink. Somebody asked me for one the other day and Flower explained it."

"I should take you both to a little Drazen place in the food court that serves real mixed drinks. It's always open during jumps. When do you get off work?"

"Pass," Julie said, Bill echoing her a second later.

"Don't know what you're missing," Jorb said, dumping the whole bottle of hot sauce on his meatloaf. Then he made an indent in his mashed potatoes and added a generous shot of vodka.

"Minor point of interest," Flower said to the captain over his implant when he paused to glance back at the

52

diner. "I wouldn't normally bother you with this, but you're going to hear about it anyway."

"I saw the lights flicker," Woojin said. "Did you make an unexpected course change?"

"We encountered a navigation hazard and I had to employ my secondary asteroid repulsion system."

"Didn't you tell me that you can go thousands of years at a stretch without encountering any space debris big enough to cause damage?"

"It wasn't exactly debris. More like three armed ships."

"Were these the same ships that attacked us last cycle? Did you destroy them?"

"They could be friends of the Bitters so I settled for punching them in the nose," Flower said. "I didn't want to bother you while you were chatting, but I thought I should mention it in case you see the video on the Grenouthian news again and get upset that I didn't tell you."

"I'm the captain, Flower. I'm even wearing the hat. I realize there may not have been time to call me to the bridge, but you could have at least informed me beforehand. And how is it that the Grenouthian network keeps getting the footage?"

"Thanks to my open Stryxnet connection to Union Station, I sell it to them. You wouldn't believe what they pay me for a few seconds of ship-to-ship combat video."

"Lume," Woojin addressed a four-armed alien, who was buttoning up a heavy overcoat as he headed around the back of the ice cream place. "On your way to debriefing a field agent?"

"I really wish you could talk Flower into a better privacy arrangement for us than a walk-in freezer," the Dollnick intelligence agent responded. "I've read a little about your history and I'm beginning to feel like a cold war spy."

Five

"Where are you going, Irene?" Harry asked, as his wife rose from the lunch table with her tray immediately after finishing off the healthy bean-based dessert. "We're having a board meeting and I thought you wanted to sit in."

"I was shopping at the bazaar today while you were baking for aliens and I saw an announcement about training to be an information desk volunteer. I checked with Flower and it will cover my community service requirement."

"Do you mean you'll be volunteering at the library with Nancy?"

"No, I'm talking about the information desks at the amusement park and the bazaar. You wouldn't believe how many people visiting the ship for the day get lost."

"I'd believe it. Does that mean you're going to have to memorize where everything is?"

"I've been shopping here for almost two months, Harry. I'll bet I know the bazaar better than some of the vendors who work there. And I can always ask Flower for help pointing people in the right direction in the amusement park or the food court. Visitors to the ship don't realize that talking to her is even an option."

"I don't think Flower can hear us over the crowds in the amusement park or the bazaar. But I guess if you're at an information desk..."

"If I pass the test I can also become a roving greeter. You must have seen greeters in those cute smocks walking around helping people in the public areas."

"I hadn't noticed," Harry confessed. "Don't work too hard."

"I won't," Irene said. She carried her tray to the bus cart before leaving the common room.

"Couldn't talk her into staying?" Brenda asked, taking the seat Irene had just vacated. "I thought she'd have good input for us about creating group activities because she's so social. Your wife is one of the friendliest people I've ever met."

"Irene always took care of the counter at our bakery, and she would have stayed for the meeting, but she signed up for a volunteer job. Have you figured out your own community service yet?"

"I'm with legal aid," the retired attorney said. "It's actually a lot of fun because most of the questions I get are related to alien laws that I don't know anything about."

"Is that helpful to people?"

"It's the best advice they can expect for free," Brenda said. "Besides, I'm learning on the job."

"Any idea where the others are?"

"We're early. I'd guess they haven't eaten yet or they went elsewhere, but I'm sure they'll be here."

"I have a legal question," Flower announced out of the blue. Harry and Brenda both looked up at the speaker grille above their table in surprise. "What? Did you think I know everything?"

"Pretty much," Harry said. "You're almost twenty thousand years old and you were probably a lot smarter than us to start with."

"Smart enough not to act as my own lawyer. It's a hypothetical question."

"About a friend?" Brenda asked, rolling her eyes at Harry on hearing the AI pull out the oldest ploy in the book.

"Yes. Imagine a Dollnick colony ship, no, a trade vessel, visiting a planet leased by Humans that doesn't have an established government."

"They'd all kill each other," Harry commented.

"Say they don't because they're too busy playing games," Flower continued. "And say there was a business on the colony ship—"

"Trade vessel," Brenda interrupted.

"Right, on the trade vessel, that arranged to deliver cash-on-delivery packages for a repair depot on the planet. And say the repair depot demanded to get paid upfront before handing over the packages."

"For the full value of the eventual collections?"

"I bargained them down to ten percent."

"This isn't hypothetical."

"The point is, I suspect the repair depot inflated the potential value of the collections and created false cash-on-delivery tags for the packages to deceive me. Is there anything in Human law that gives me grounds to get my apples back?"

"Is that a Dollnick expression for money?" Brenda asked.

"You don't think I paid cash, do you? I wasn't born yesterday."

"Why apples?"

"Because they wouldn't accept plums or pears. Bartering fresh fruit is trickier than I thought."

"Bits is an anarchy, and if they're smart, they've already eaten the apples," Brenda said. "How much do you think they inflated the true value by?"

"Probably a thousand percent, but that's not the real issue. I had Dewey scan all of the labels for me, and it appears that at least some of the addressees are as fake as the amounts."

"You mean they made it all up?"

"Unless there's a Donald Duck living on Timble," Flower said grimly. "A Bugs Bunny I might have believed."

Brenda started laughing and covered her face with her hands.

"What's so funny?" Harry demanded. "So they're both ancient cartoon characters."

"Bunnies," Brenda managed, tears rolling down her cheeks. "Timble is a Grenouthian orbital."

"Flower made a joke?"

"It's not funny if it has to be explained," the Dollnick AI said. "If there's no legal recourse, let's just keep this a little secret among the three of us, shall we?"

"Don't you think anybody else heard?" Harry said, looking around at the other members of the independent living cooperative who were finishing their lunches at nearby tables.

"No, I'm very good with acoustics."

"I still can't believe you got taken in by a bunch of hackers."

"This may come as a surprise to you, but I've realized that I have limited experience dealing with Humans who aren't living on board my ship. I've discussed this with my Stryx mentor, and she pointed out that in my usual business arrangements with your people, I've been negotiating from a position of power."

"Like changing the name of our independent living cooperative after we had already picked one, and refusing to serve ice cream at every meal," Brenda enumerated.

"Exactly. There are things I know that I know, and things I know that I don't know, but this was a case where I thought I knew something that I didn't. It won't happen again."

"What won't happen again?" Jack asked. He pulled out a chair for Nancy to sit and then took his seat next to her. "Did we miss something?"

"My catering service didn't bring enough plates for all the new members," Flower lied smoothly. "Fortunately, you and Nancy chose to eat elsewhere today, and Dave is on a diet. Have some fruit."

"Thank you, it's lovely," Nancy said, taking a ripe plum from the bowl on the table.

"Where did you two go for lunch?" Brenda asked the new arrivals.

"A little Italian place in the food court owned by a friend I worked with decades ago," Jack said. "He opens for lunch on Tuesdays, Wednesdays, and Fridays while Flower is underway. I'm trying to recruit him for the cooperative."

"Somehow, I don't think that dangling me in front of him will be enough," Nancy added, and winked at Brenda.

"I may have a lead on new members if you can run some ads on Trume Six, Flower," Jack said. "My friend recently heard from an acquaintance who was part of our first contract labor group to work for the Dollnicks, and his current group just finished up a terraforming job ahead of time."

"Trume Six?" Flower asked. "I keep up with all of our terraforming projects and there haven't been any announcements about a schedule change. It's been in the final landscaping stage for the last sixty years, and the inspection tours for potential buyers don't start for another four cycles."

"The work crew's contract has three cycles left to run, but the job is already finished, and they're getting paid to rake beaches and mow prairie grass just to keep everybody busy. According to my friend, the only reason the workers haven't been moved to a new project is that the Dollnick managers are trying to keep it quiet."

"Why wouldn't they want everybody to know that they finished a job ahead of schedule?" Brenda asked.

"Because it means that their estimates were off and they hired more workers than necessary," Flower explained. "Dollnicks pride themselves on managing large construction projects, and any deviation from the original schedule means that somebody made a mistake."

"Where is Dave?" Nancy asked.

"He's on his way here now. It's easier for him to stick to his diet if he doesn't have to watch everybody else eating lunch."

"How about breakfast and dinner?" Harry asked.

"They're not part of the diet. It's just lunch."

"I don't think that will work."

"M793qK and I came up with the plan, and Dave has reduced his caloric intake by a little more than the five-hundred calories a day we targeted."

"You know that most people cheat on diets," Brenda said. "They might not even be aware of it themselves."

"I'd know," Flower asserted. "My infrared sensors are well suited to monitoring the heat created by your digestive tracts."

"I'm glad I missed the first part of that conversation," Maureen said, taking the seat next to Harry and placing her large display tab on the table. "I've done some story-boarding for the new ads if we have time to look at them. If not, I'll just go over it with Flower later."

"Sorry I'm late," a slightly out-of-breath man with a pot belly apologized, taking the last seat. "I just got back from walking a full circumference of the deck. Last month I would have laughed if you told me I could ever make it that far on my own feet."

"That was before the doctor redid your knee and you started exercising again," Nancy said. "It's surprising even to me how much we can still do if we put our minds to it."

"Which is why I asked you to set aside two hours for this meeting," Jack said, his voice now all business. "I know it may feel like I'm rushing things, but I want to launch the activities we've been advertising as quickly as possible so we can get the bugs out before we get too big. But first, we have a stack of applications to go through."

"How many?" Harry asked.

"A hundred and fifty-three, but we only have to get through a dozen today. Flower has been pre-screening for obvious mismatches, like people who are too young, or who express a fear of alien artificial intelligence."

"That's on the applications?"

"It seemed prudent," the Dollnick AI informed them.

"What's so special about a dozen?" Dave asked.

"That's how many were submitted from Timble, our next stop," Jack explained. "Flower responded to the rest of the inquiries for us, telling them that their applications are under active consideration and they'll hear back soon."

"So what are we screening for if Flower has already gone through them?" Harry asked. "It's not like we're hiring them for a job."

"That's a valid point," Brenda agreed. "If they pass Flower's criteria and they can afford to pay, who are we to turn their money away?"

"The management," Jack said. "Remember, we're the ones with our names on the prospectus, and our members are counting on us to make decisions that will preserve the nature of our cooperative. Maybe we won't encounter any problems, but don't you think that independent living facilities on Earth at least read the applications before taking people's money?"

"I doubt it, but we're here, so we may as well take a look," Harry said. "Did you have them printed?"

"They're all on my tab," Maureen said. "I'll just read them off and show you the video."

"They had to provide video of themselves?" Nancy asked.

"It's a good way to check the veracity of their statements," Flower explained. "While I may open an assisted living facility and a nursing home in the future, for the time being Flower's Paradise can only accept people who are in good enough shape to take care of themselves. I have several years of experience in putting Humans through their paces, and I can tell a lot about a person's health from the way they walk."

"But what if they submit video of somebody else?"

There was a pause before Flower asked, "Would they really do that?"

"I tried a video dating service after my divorce, and if the video of the men I met wasn't of somebody else, it must have been shot long before I met them," Nancy said.

"I think we're safe with these," Maureen said. "There are four couples and four singles applying, but three of the singles are sisters. They're all professionals, by the way, so they'd be great for producing new commercials."

"Professional whats?"

"Performers. The sisters have a song-and-dance act, and they go under the name of the Barry Girls. Check this out." Maureen spun her tab around and tilted it up so everybody at the table could see. Then she said, "Play."

Three women dressed in matching skirts and berets that brought to mind military uniforms performed a song and dance number before introducing themselves and giving their ages. All three of them turned out to be fifteen years older than they looked.

"What's a Boogie Woogie Bugle Boy?" Harry couldn't help asking.

"Military companies once employed buglers for communications," Nancy told them. "I'm pretty sure that the routine we just saw was from a World War Two era movie. It makes sense if they're on Timble for the theme park, but I thought it wasn't open yet."

"It says in their application that they've been working in Grenouthian documentaries for the last two decades and they're ready for retirement," Maureen said. "The youngest of the sisters is a year older than me, and as healthy as they look, I can't imagine that putting on multiple performances a day in a theme park could be any fun at that age."

"Did they fill in the section about their expectations?" Jack asked.

Maureen turned the tab back around and read, "Two of us have outlived our husbands, and Jeanie hasn't seen hers for a decade since he ran off with a magician's assistant.

We're impressed with the active lifestyle offered by Flower's Paradise, and we're hoping to meet our volunteering requirement by sharing the music and dance we've always loved."

"Sold," Harry said. "That's three new members."

"I hope they're all like this," Nancy said. "I'd hate to have to reject somebody."

"So here's the other single," Maureen said, spinning her tab back around and tilting it up again. "Play."

A woman whose entire body was encased in a shiny black skin-tight suit that might have been artificial leather took a step forward in stiletto heels and tapped a riding crop against her leg. She leered at the camera and demanded, "Who's a bad boy?"

"No," Nancy said. "Fail, fail, fail."

"Maybe she's just lonely," Dave protested.

"Fail," Brenda said. "How did she get past the screening, Flower?"

"Her cash balance is substantial and her health appears to be good," the Dollnick AI replied. "Is it her outfit you object to?"

"What did she write about her expectations?" Jack asked.

"I'm looking forward to new worlds and men to conquer," Maureen read, unable to suppress a chuckle. "She seems confident in her abilities."

"I don't want to sound like a prude, but I went through this with my ex," Nancy said. "Let's just pass on this one."

The four applications from couples were quickly approved, and Jack immediately returned to the subject of group activities. "Maureen and I have reviewed all of our ads that have run to date, and we made up a list of the implied promises. We're already covered for the events managed by Flower, like our catered meals, the morning calisthenics, the team sport, and the volunteering, but we're behind on the lifetime learning classes, the dancing, and the hobbies."

"You forgot the tour group at the stops," Dave said.

"It doesn't seem right to count it while we're taking advantage of the stops to recruit more members."

"As soon as we pick up the Barry Girls we'll be set on singing and dancing," Maureen said. "Flower can pipe in music for practice, and there should be no trouble finding an ensemble on board to play when we're ready for a formal dance."

"Why don't you tell everybody about the classes you've been working up?" Jack suggested to Nancy.

"Well, nothing is carved in stone yet, but I've been canvassing our current members for suggestions. Some of the ideas are better suited to informal groups than classes, like a book club and a knitting circle, and we could have them right here if Flower would agree to shorten the legs on the Dollnick couches and easy chairs she brought in."

"Cutting down the legs is the last resort," the AI told them. "I'll have a few maintenance bots return the normal-sized furniture to storage this afternoon and find some Human-sized replacements."

"Thank you. When it comes to classes, I was a bit surprised by the requests. The most popular topics were galactic current events and galactic geography, followed by Earth history. I could teach the last one, but I'm afraid we'll have to hire instructors for the first two, unless somebody in the cooperative has the knowledge and desire."

"We could ask Dianne, the reporter, if she'll teach galactic current events," Brenda suggested. "Even though she was an entertainment correspondent before coming here, I think she's very well informed."

"Galactic geography sounds funny," Dave said. "Are you sure geography isn't limited to Earth by definition?"

"I'm sure it once was, but words change meaning over time, and it kept coming up in conversations. Many of us have family spread throughout the tunnel network, and it would be nice to learn a little about the places that their messages are sent from," Nancy said. "My niece and her husband are living on Corner Station, but their children have all left for worlds in the Conference of Sovereign Human Communities."

"I can teach galactic geography," Flower offered. "How much were you planning to pay instructors?"

"We were hoping for volunteers," Jack said. "If you could count their teaching time against your community service requirement..."

"Am I a charity now? My advice is to charge a fee for the classes because the students won't take it seriously otherwise. The fees can go to the room rental and the teacher."

"I thought we'd just hold classes in here after meals," Jack said.

"That's fine for a cooperative with fifty members, but I hope to see us at five hundred by the next time we stop at Earth, and I have a two-year plan to get to five thousand. If we're going to be able to scale quickly, you need to do all of your planning with that expansion in mind."

"Flower's right about charging at least a token amount for classes and guest lectures, I was going to suggest that myself," Nancy said. "And I can tell you from my own teaching days that there never seem to be enough class-rooms, so it's a good idea to be prepared."

"Guest lectures?" Harry asked.

"I thought it would be interesting to bring in speakers for a weekly lecture series, including aliens. Some of the most interesting speakers I saw back on Earth had backgrounds in business and entertainment rather than academia or politics. It's always easy to find college professors and politicians willing to talk about their pet subjects, but I like hearing first-hand accounts from travelers and people who have dedicated their lives to their passions."

"So the dominatrix is back in?" Dave asked.

"Not that sort of passions."

Six

"What's this?" Lume asked Bill, who approached the table and extended a plate.

"Compliments of the chef. He's trying dessert recipes from the All Species Cookbook."

"That was fast. The new edition published by Humans was just released."

"Dollnick Intelligence spies on cooks?"

"The cookbook is a bigger deal than you may realize. The previous editions have come close to causing wars." Lume chose one of the round black objects with yellow and green inclusions from the proffered plate, knocked it against the metal table, and then made a show of checking for a dent.

"I'll try one," Jorb said. "Everybody knows that Dollnicks have weak teeth."

"Are you sure it doesn't have flour?" Razood asked his part-time apprentice.

"Harry said it meets everybody's dietary restrictions and they'll keep for months in a cookie tin," Bill responded. "They actually smell pretty good."

The Drazen bit into the cookie and made a face. "Too sweet."

Both the Frunge and the Dollnick took that as a positive indication and sampled their own cookies.

"Not terrible," Lume said, using his boarding house reach to snag a couple more cookies from the plate with one of his upper arms. "The green bits remind me of algae."

"I think they're colored candy of some sort," Razood ventured. "These really aren't that bad for something that everyone can eat."

"Who brought cookies?" a stunning Vergallian woman inquired as she took the seat next to the Dollnick. "Is it somebody's Naming Day?"

"Harry is experimenting with the new All Species Cookbook desserts," Bill explained. "I'll just leave the plate here."

"I thought the captain called us together for a debriefing," Lume said, as Bill returned to the kitchen. "Where is he?"

"I passed him on my way here from the lift tube," Avisia said. "He was walking with Brynlan."

The other aliens all let out a groan on hearing that Woojin was accompanying the slow-footed and even slower-spoken Verlock. Then a giant bunny entered the cafeteria and took a seat at the table. He eyed the cookies with suspicion.

"Go ahead, Director," Jorb said. "They're too sweet for my taste."

"Everything that wouldn't dissolve this table top is too sweet for your taste," the Grenouthian shot back, but he took a cookie in his furry paw and nibbled a bit off the edge. "Edible."

"You seem to be in a particularly cheerful mood today."

"I've been contacted by the biggest production company on Timble and they want to interview me for a job."

"Directing immersive documentaries?"

"They wouldn't have paid for a tunneling call to offer me a position as a third grip."

"Congratulations," Jorb said, thumping the bunny on the back. "It's what you've always dreamed of."

"This calls for a drink," Lume added, getting up and heading for the bar. "Who's joining me?"

"Divverflip," Jorb said.

"I'll have one of those bubbly Human drinks," the bunny requested.

"Champagne?" the Dollnick asked, pulling on a pair of heavy rubber gloves as a precaution before mixing the Drazen's toxic beverage.

"The one for working stiffs, like me."

"You mean beer," the Vergallian woman said. "It's not as good as their wine, but it has a certain authenticity that I enjoy. Some of our royal families have started brewing their own."

"I think I saw a box of them here somewhere," Lume said. He finished adding a measured quantity of acid to the Divverflip and then gave it another dash from the bottle. "Come and take this, Jorb. I don't want to risk sloshing it on myself."

"Who keeps adult beverages in a box?" the Grenouthian asked. "I've seen their children drinking from waxed paper containers with a straw, but they didn't look suitable for high volume consumption."

"I've tried Human wine in boxes and you're better off taking a pass," Avisia added.

"You must have drunk beer in taverns where it comes out of a barrel," Lume told the Grenouthian. He reached with his lower arms and fished a six-pack of cans out of the back of the bar fridge. "Humans distribute retail quantities of beer in bottles or cans, and if you buy enough, you get a box as well."

"Are we celebrating something?" Woojin asked, entering the small cafeteria with his shuffling Verlock companion. "I'll have a beer if you're buying, Lume."

"In a manner of speaking, you're the one buying," the Dollnick replied. "Keeping the cafeteria bar stocked is one of the benefits EarthCent Intelligence grants alien agents in return for our cooperation."

"The business stuff is above my pay grade but I'll gladly accept a beer. What brand is it?"

"Is there more than one kind?"

"There are thousands of brands. Maybe tens of thousands. A friend of mine on Union Station brews his own at home and sells it to restaurants."

"He must have a large cabin or a small family," the Grenouthian observed.

"Joe's got one of the largest private spaces on the station, right on the core," Woojin explained. "It used to be a junkyard, but now they run it as a ship repair facility, and they recently started a rental agency."

"Here you go," Lume said, bringing six cans on a tray to the table and placing it in the center. The aliens all stared at the cans with the flip-top tabs, and even the Dollnick appeared to be puzzled. "So how do we get the beer out, Captain?"

"Allow me." Woojin took one of the cans and expertly popped the tab with an index finger. Beer sprayed all over him and the Verlock who was just taking the final seat, and Lume let out a shrill whistle of glee.

"Works every time," the Dollnick crowed, making a vigorous shaking motion with one of his hands. "Don't worry," he added for the benefit of the others. "I only shook that one and positioned the tray so he would take it. Humans are so predictable."

The Grenouthian held one hand close to his can as a furry shield while popping the tab, but the only thing to escape was some carbonation.

"Am I supposed to drink it out of this?"

"I'll bring some glasses while I'm getting a towel," Woojin said, casting a nasty look at the chortling Dollnick. "Do you want anything, Brynlan?"

"Is there jerky?"

"I'll ask in the kitchen." Just as the captain was stepping towards the swinging door, the light above it changed colors. He backed off as the door swung towards him and Bill emerged with a large platter of fruit slices and citrus wedges. Woojin slipped through the door while it was still open.

"Flower said that you're drinking and to bring munchies," Bill informed the aliens. "The food is going to be a while."

"Sounds like something went wrong," Razood observed.

"Harry said he's making Kadoodle and—"

"No thanks," the blacksmith interrupted. "I'll just stop out for something later."

"Same here," Lume chimed in.

"Me too," the Vergallian said.

"Done right, it's disgusting," Jorb added. "Done wrong, it's deadly."

"Won't anybody try it?" Bill asked.

"No, and you wouldn't either if you'd ever had it before," Razood said. "Remember when I took you to Flower's foundry and we melted down some scrap metal?"

"Sure, that was just a few days ago."

"And I had you skim the scum off the top?"

"Dross, you called it."

"Kadoodle is like that, only chewier."

"I better tell Harry the Kadoodle is a no-go," Bill said, almost running into the captain, who had already reemerged from the kitchen.

"Is Kadoodle really that bad?" Woojin asked, handing the Verlock a package of jerky along with a dish towel.

"I'll put it this way," Lume said. "It's from an old edition of the All Species Cookbook that was published in a version of Universal that AI's like Flower try to translate for fun. Here," he added, offering the captain the last beer.

Woojin peered at the Dollnick suspiciously, tapped on the top of the can with his fingernails, and then shielding it with his off-hand the way the bunny had, popped the tab without any ill effects.

"If we're all done playing games, I'm teaching the girls ballroom dancing this evening so I can't stay long," the Vergallian said. "Any volunteers for waltz partners?" The aliens all found somewhere else to look, and the proprietress of the finishing school sniffed loudly. "How about you, M793qK?"

The giant beetle, who had arrived late to the party, didn't deign to answer. He picked up one of the cookies, examined it through his multifaceted eyes, and then set it back on the plate.

"I asked you all here today to get your thoughts about the emigrants from Bits who we're transporting to destinations unknown," Woojin said. "I'm sure you know that the population there does business with the pirates, and my chief of security has his people talking with as many of the Bitters as possible. We want to determine if there's any information they're willing to share."

72

"Offer money," the Grenouthian interjected.

"We're saving that for our fallback position."

"How many came aboard in the end?" Lume asked. "I heard it was going to be around twenty thousand."

"Nineteen thousand, eight hundred and six," Flower contributed.

"How come you wouldn't tell me that when I asked?" the captain demanded.

The Verlock nudged Woojin to get his attention and pointed at the top of his own leathery skull to indicate the captain's missing headgear.

"Lynx brought my tricorn hat to the cleaners and it's the only one I have," the captain complained to the ceiling. "You have to be reasonable, Flower."

"I don't have to be anything, but I'll let it slide this time," the Dollnick AI responded. "I took advantage of the cameras I had installed while Julie was being stalked to examine all of our guests from Bits as they boarded. Then I ran their images against the ISPOA database. Three hundred and nineteen have criminal records, but only eleven show outstanding warrants, and I passed that information on to your chief of security just a few minutes ago."

"Will we be given an opportunity to interrogate them?" the Vergallian asked.

"I'm sure something could be arranged."

"I mean, without having to pay."

"In that case, you'll have access to the report filed with ISPOA," Flower replied. "Taken as a whole, the Bitters are as serviceable a group of Humans as I've come across, and I'm interested in keeping as many as possible."

"By keeping, you mean you want them to move onto the ship permanently?" Woojin asked.

"Why not? Do you have something against computer geeks?"

"No. Well, maybe, but that's not the point. I'm aware that you have ample capacity to absorb ten times that number—"

"Two hundred times."

"—but I'm worried about socialization problems. We're talking about people who have dedicated their lives to playing old computer games and programming obsolete hardware. They come from a hacking tradition in which breaking the rules is a virtue rather than a vice."

"That's very poetical of you, Captain Hatless, but they'll quickly find that hacking sentient AI is out of their league. More importantly, these Bitters have an interest in holographic programming that I'd like to encourage. Rendering holograms is tedious work, even for AI. That's why creating three-dimensional animations is typically a job that falls to the latest up-and-coming sentients who need the exchange currency."

"Your plan is to draft all of the Bitters into making three-dimensional cartoons?" Woojin demanded.

"You make it sound unethical," Flower complained. "My Stryx mentor thought it was a splendid idea, and I could use both the population boost and the hard currency."

"We got out of the animation business millions of years ago because of the labor involved," the Grenouthian commented. "The last I heard our studios were going off the tunnel network to find animators."

"I thought all the work was done by computers," Woojin said.

"All of the work is never done by computers," Flower told him. "That's the difference between computers and artificial intelligence. Computers can only execute tasks that are defined to the point that you may as well do the work yourself."

"You're exaggerating, and I have to go," the Vergallian said, crushing her empty beer can and tossing it into the recycling bin. "If you do get any useful intelligence about the pirates out of the Bitters, Captain, I expect to be informed."

"But wouldn't you need artists for an animation business?" Woojin asked Flower after Avisia sashayed out.

"You don't know much about games, for a Human. For every programmer working on the physics engine, there are ninety-nine plotting storylines and doing artwork. The Bitters are a perfect match, and possession is nine-tenths of the law."

"I've heard that one," Harry said, stalking up to the table. "Bill told me none of you are willing to try the Kadoodle."

"Did Flower really put you through the whole process of weaving the dough helix and flame hardening the top?" Jorb asked.

"I know how to follow a recipe. I thought it would be fun to try something from one of the old editions of the All Species Cookbook and Flower offered to translate for me."

"Kadoodle was originally based on a Drazen recipe that's as difficult to eat as it is to make," Jorb told him. "But what really ruins it is the ingredient substitutions. The Kadoodle comes out looking all right, but it's indigestible. It was only in the All Species Cookbook because the Hortens edited the last edition and they wanted to make us look bad."

"I'll have a slice," Brynlan said slowly.

The other aliens turned to the Verlock in surprise, and he gave them a slow wink on the side of his face turned away from the baker.

"At least one of you is a good sport," Harry said and turned back towards the kitchen. "I'll bring a slice right out."

"Ten creds we don't see him again tonight," Jorb said.

"I hope he didn't bring his good knives," Razood added. "Bill, tell him that I can repair any damage."

"I take it that Kadoodle doesn't slice easily," Woojin guessed.

"Not unless you have a plasma cutter," Jorb said.

"I wonder who's going to manage the animation business?" the Grenouthian mused.

"I was planning on you, but if you quit the ship at Timble, it will have to be me," Flower told him bluntly. "While my ultimate goal is creating a large contract studio to provide suitable employment for the Bitters and keep them on board, in the short run, we have a marketing problem."

"What's that?" Woojin asked.

"Have you ever heard of Flower Studios?"

"No, but from what my wife tells me, you've done so well with marketing Flower's Paradise that the cooperative's committee is running behind on reviewing applications."

"Independent living is an easy product to sell," the Dollnick AI explained. "The three major points of the value proposition are the food, the lodging, and the people, all of which are in place and are easy to show off with advertising. I don't expect major animation producers to start sending me work just because I announce that I'm in business. What I need—"

"—is a completed production to showcase," the Grenouthian director interjected. "My first choice remains directing documentaries on Timble, but it doesn't hurt to have a backup plan. Will you give me full autonomy?"

"No," Flower snapped.

"It never hurts to ask. Do you have a story or a script?"

"I was thinking about something with a mixed-species team of superheroes. I'm counting on you all for volunteer consulting."

"But my position will be paid," the bunny stated.

"I'll double the salary Eccentric Enterprises has been paying you for running the community theatre project, but I'll expect you to work three times as hard."

"How many points do I get?"

"You want me to score your answer?"

"Points in the production. No self-respecting Grenouthian director could agree to a project without getting a percentage. The director normally gets ten points."

"Five," Flower responded immediately.

"Done," the bunny said, slapping his belly with glee.

"Methinks somebody may have answered a little too quickly," Woojin chortled, amused to finally see the aliens taking advantage of somebody other than himself.

"And methinks our furry friend is forgetting something," Flower shot back. "Who do you think will be keeping the books for this production?"

"What do you mean?" the captain asked.

"The Grenouthian points system is based on net profits."

"But five percent is still five percent."

"Flower isn't going into the production business to make a profit, she just wants to market her animation studios," Lume explained.

"I get to audit the books," the bunny growled. "All three sets."

"What will you want from the rest of us?" the Verlock spy asked slowly.

"Script consulting and help with character development," Flower answered him. "I have access to an extensive library of animated entertainment, but I admit that the popular taste eludes me."

"I've always found you to be pretty down-to-earth for an AI," Woojin said. "Can you give us an example of what you mean?"

"Take the reliance on unsympathetic characters. Why do you all watch dramas about people you wouldn't want as friends?"

"To create tension," the director explained. "That's why nobody has ever produced a drama set on a Stryx station. There's no way to ratchet up the stakes when the station management knows what the villains are planning before they know themselves. It would be like reading a mystery without a murder."

"What's wrong with everything working out for the best?" Flower demanded. "I've watched every episode of 'Let's Make Friends' and—"

"That's a show for little children," the Grenouthian interrupted. "You need to have heroes and villains if you want to get older viewers hooked on your production. And the characters have to have flaws."

"Like Humans and their limited math skills?" Brynlan rumbled.

"Amateurs," the director cried, throwing his arms up in the air. "I'm talking about character flaws, like lying and cheating or being addicted to drugs and alcohol. How do you keep the lovers apart until the end of a romance if you don't keep throwing obstacles between them?"

"Why keep them apart?" Flower asked. "Wouldn't it make more sense to bring them together right at the start so everybody could watch them building a family and contributing to society in a positive way?"

"You're confusing life with entertainment. Forget about your desire to micromanage everything on board for the best outcome and think in terms of what's going to keep their butts in seats."

"Safety restraints?" Lume ventured.

"Laugh all you want, but there's a lot more to this business than any of you can imagine," the Grenouthian growled. "And in the exceedingly unlikely chance I don't take the job on Timble, my price just went up."

"Fighting is always popular in dramas," Razood said. "I can be the weapons consultant, and Jorb can handle the fight choreography."

"Anything to get some new sign-ups for the dojo," the Drazen agreed.

"But there won't be any real weapons to consult on or fighters to train," Woojin protested. "Flower just explained that it's all going to be done by the animation artists and programmers from Bits she's going to hire."

"I've just started negotiating with them," Flower admitted. "There are still plenty of details to hash out, but I think for my first production it would be wise to accommodate myself to their standard practices as much as possible."

79

Seven

"Think you're up to covering the main desk for the final hour before lunch?" Bea asked.

Julie looked at the head librarian in surprise. "Do you mean completely by myself, with nobody else around? Where will you all be?"

"The community that came aboard at Bits brought an extensive digital library with them and they're interested in licensing us a copy. I have mixed feelings about getting involved with electronic books, but we're having a meeting to give them a fair hearing. Dewey and I are gathering the rest of the staff in the reading room for a presentation, so if there's an emergency, you can ask Flower to ping us."

"I'll be fine," Julie said. "Oh, just in case, can you show me how to access the *For Humans* collection? I know where it is, but the panel won't open for me."

"Ask Dewey," Bea replied and stalked away in a huff.

"You know that she hates those books," the AI assistant librarian said. He motioned for Julie to follow him to the blank section of bulkhead where the popular collection of *For Humans* books was kept under lock and key. "The code is 'Open Sesame.'"

"Open Sesame," Julie said uncertainly.

"No, you have to send it electronically. Basic machine messaging is built into your implant."

"It is? Nobody told me. How do I do it?"

"You should be able to access the menu via your heads-up display, but I need to get to the meeting, so ask Flower for the details," Dewey said. "See you after the presentation."

"Flower?" Julie subvoced, her lips barely moving.

"I didn't tell you about the heads-up display because I thought it would be too much for you to take in all at once," the Dollnick AI replied defensively.

"But what is a heads-up display? I've never even heard of one."

"Maybe you should go back to the circulation desk and sit down. I understand it can be very disorienting the first time you use one."

"I remember you telling the Farling doctor to give me a high-quality implant. Am I the only person on the ship to have one?"

"The ship's officers have diplomatic grade implants from Union Station, and most of the alien businessmen are equipped with the top versions from their own species. Dianne's implant was supplied by the Galactic Free Press, and I'm sure that either she or Lynx would be willing to coach you if the help screens aren't sufficient."

"What do I do?" Julie asked, sitting down on the high stool behind the circulation desk.

"Invoke the 'heads-up' command."

"How do I do that?"

"Concentrate on the words."

"Something seemed to flash in front of my eyes but then it vanished."

"You got distracted. Try again."

"I—oh, wow," Julie said, gaping at the dense text that suddenly overlaid her vision. "Is it always like this? I'd fall over if I tried to walk."

"Are you giving me permission to access what you're seeing?"

"Yes. I mean—"

"I've added myself as a registered user," Flower cut her off. "That's the Eula. You have to scroll down to the bottom and agree to the terms."

"What's a Eula?"

"End User License Agreement."

"How do I scroll? Ohhh," Julie moaned, sagging forward as the text raced past in a blur. "How do I stop it?"

"The implant tracks your eye movements from the nerve impulses and pans the display area to match. Just get to the bottom and look directly at the 'accept' button."

"But I haven't read it."

"Nobody in the history of your species has ever read a Eula. Are you going to throw up? There's a bin under the counter."

"No, I just went too fast. I accept," Julie said, mentally punching the button. "Wait, everything went away!"

"As it should, but your heads-up display is now enabled should you call on its functionality."

"What's it good for?"

"Distraction, mainly. Here," Flower said, and a menu appeared before the girl's eyes. Before Julie could even read the options, the Dollnick AI took over and navigated through a series of submenus until another 'accept' button popped up and was accepted. Then the front page of the free version of the Galactic Free Press was suddenly superimposed over her vision.

"Ugh. I don't think I could get used to this."

"Try closing your eyes so you can see the heads-up display without any background."

"Oh, that's not so bad. Whoa," she cried, leaning forward to catch her balance as the stories began blurring past.

"Stop trying to look for the bottom of the text or it will always do that. Pretend you're reading from a book."

"This is going to take some getting used to."

"Which is why I suggest you practice in the comfort of your room rather than at work," Flower said. "There's a very patient young man standing in front of the desk waiting for you to open your eyes."

"Sorry," she said reflexively, turning to look at the patron, and losing her balance as the virtual newspaper and the real world moved in opposite directions. "Turn it off, Flower."

The heads-up display vanished, and Julie reached out for the desk with both hands to reestablish her balance.

"Did I wake you?" the young man asked with a grin.

"No. I just found out I have a heads-up display and I was practicing, sort of."

"You have a high-grade implant? I've always wanted to get one but they were considered tacky on Bits, not that I could have afforded the cost in any case. Working at a library must pay better than I thought."

"It's a long story," Julie said, already regretting that she had shared such personal information with a stranger. "Can I help you?"

"I heard that this library might actually have the best collection of twentieth-century Earth classics anywhere in the galaxy. I've read all of the really important books in electronic form, but I've always wondered what it would be like to actually hold the original text."

"You've come to the right place. Did you have any particular titles in mind?"

"Do you have Kernighan and Ritchie?"

"Is that a title or two authors?"

"Two authors. C."

"See? I guess."

"You guess you have it?"

"I meant I could see it being two authors."

The young man looked at her funny. "The C Programming Language. It's like the foundational text."

"C as in the letter 'C'?"

"Yes."

"Let me check." Julie tapped the library catalog tab to life and entered the title. "Wow, it looks like we have a whole stack."

The young man grinned and extended his hand. "You got me, code girl. I'm Zick."

"Julie," she said, giving a perfunctory handshake. "What's a code girl?"

"Come on, that 'stack' line was too perfect. You're a programmer yourself, aren't you?"

"I can barely even operate technology beyond my old teacher bot. The only programming I've ever done is picking out books for the children's reading hour."

"So you were serious about the K&R?"

"Excuse me?"

"Kernighan and Ritchie. Do you really have a, uh, pile of them?"

"According to my tab, we have more than it makes sense to shelve. You can probably take a copy to keep, though I'll have to check with one of the regular staff, and they're all in a meeting right now. I'm just an intern."

"That's my mom's meeting. She's trying to license the library a copy of our archives, and charging a token amount is just a trick to get them to accept it for the sake of additional backup. My mom's a bit nuts about making copies."

"How come you aren't at the meeting?"

"I came to carry the display she's using but I'm not that into electronic books. Are you seeing anybody?"

"C'ing? Is that a programming thing?"

"You know, like dating. Maybe I could buy you a meal and you could show me around the station if you aren't hooked up already."

"No, not like you mean, but I just met you. Is everybody from Bits so—"

"Aggressive?" Zick interrupted. "We all spent half of our lives playing games, if not more. After you've died a few thousand times, getting shot down asking a girl for a date doesn't seem like that big of a risk."

"I always heard it went the other way around, though I've never really known any, uh, tech types."

"Geeks. It's nothing to be ashamed of, and everybody on Bits is pretty good at expressing themselves. Might be the pirate influence, you know."

"I'll have to pass on that meal for now because I have a thing about eating with strangers," Julie said. "I can't really leave the desk to show you the books because I'm the only one here. I could describe where you'll find them, but it's at least a ten-minute walk through the stacks and you'll probably get lost."

"I've got another forty-five minutes to kill while Mom makes her pitch, and I'm really good with quests."

"Quests?"

"You know, following clues to discover hidden treasures, stuff like that. Don't you game?"

"No. Our tour guide on Bits asked me the same question."

"There's nothing to see on Bits unless you're into gaming, and I know there aren't any tours."

"A girl around my age started to show us around the museum but she didn't seem to actually know what she was talking about. I think her name was Ariel."

"Ariel is on the junior rules committee and we had a thing going for a while. Showing you the scrap pile and pretending that it's a museum would be just like her."

"Why did you break up?"

"Irreconcilable differences. She's like most of the population on Bits, trying to reconstruct the golden age of computing on Earth before the Stryx showed up. I'm as big a fan of the classics as the next geek, but for me, they represent a step on the path, not a final destination. I want to prove that we can hold our own with the other species on their turf."

"Can we?"

"Not really," Zick admitted, sounding somewhat deflated. "Nobody can compete with sentient AI when it comes to coding, and I've seen some of the stuff out of the Verlock academies that's millions of years in advance of anything we could hope to do."

"The Verlocks are the oldest oxygen-breathing species on the tunnel network," Julie said. "They've been traveling the stars for over seven million years."

"And they used to make some really cool weapons. I worked on the upgrade team for Time Wars, which is one of our most popular games."

"The Verlocks have time travel?"

"No, but the gameplay is that the space-time continuum has been sabotaged and you have to chase the bad guys through hundreds of millions of years to save the universe. Whenever a time shift happens, you end up in an alien spaceship from that era with the weapons they used and everything."

"Sounds complicated. How could you simulate ancient alien technology that's way more advanced than anything we've ever created?"

"It's more about the look and feel than the physics engine," Zick said. "I don't want to get all technical, but it would be really tough to manage the scoring if we let players actually use the kind of doomsday weapons some species had. Most of them aren't around anymore to complain that we're just faking it with ray guns and cool sound effects."

"What happened to all those advanced aliens?"

Zick shrugged. "Species come, species go. The Stryx are the oldest AI I've ever heard of. Some people say that they built the tunnel network because they got tired of watching biological species go extinct and they wanted to do something about it."

"How do you know all of this? It wasn't on my teacher bot."

"The teacher bots only include the stuff that we've already figured out for ourselves," Zick said. "If you want to learn more about galactic history, you have to read alien books or play games."

"Play games?"

"Everything I just told you is from the back story for Time Wars. It rolls right after the sign-up."

"You goof! You had me thinking you were some kind of scholar!"

"So how about that coffee sometime? You can tell me all about life on Flower and I'll tell you what the pirates are really like. They come by Bits all the time."

"I'll think about it," Julie said. "If I explain where your book is, will you remember?"

"Mind like a computer," Zick said, tapping his temple. "Are the books in order?"

"The catalog number is 005.133 K399C," Julie read from the tab. "At least, that's the number in one of the Earth libraries we have on board." She frowned. "I think this is one of the college collections that was kept intact in case a human colony is willing to take it whole. If you can find shelves with a blue stripe over an orange stripe, you're in the right area. Do you have a tab?"

"Right here," Zick said, producing a foldable model from his belt pouch. "Flower provided all of us with these cool Dollnick tabs our first evening on board. See this?" he continued, tapping an icon of a keyboard. "It gives us the option to code just like we were back on Bits with an old Frunge factory controller emulating personal computers for everybody, except this is a lot faster. I wonder what we're actually running on?"

"Probably Flower herself," Julie said. "I don't know anything about artificial intelligence, but she seems to have a lot of spare capacity. Go back a screen and look for a book icon."

"This one?"

"That's the patron's version of the library catalog. If you put in the title of the book, it will draw you a map with the best route."

"This should be fun," Zick said, turning and almost bumping into an elderly woman who had come up behind him. "I'm off on a quest."

"He seemed very nice," Nancy commented to Julie. "Another one of your young men?"

"He just joined the ship at Bits and he's looking for old computer books. Did you read with the children at school this morning?"

"Yes, I just brought back the books. I have a lunch date with Jack today."

"Flower's Paradise business?"

"I hope not. Just a date to get to know each other away from the others and maybe strike up a few sparks."

"Nancy!"

"What?"

"But you're, you know."

"Old? I assure you I'm entirely aware of the fact that I'll never see the right side of seventy again, but that's no reason to stop living. Wish me luck."

Julie spent the rest of the hour organizing the returns in the temporary shelving area behind the desk. She wasn't sure whether she was relieved or not when Dewey came out of the meeting before Zick returned from his quest.

"We bought a license for the collection," the AI assistant librarian announced. "It was so inexpensive that I would have taken it myself if the library hadn't been willing. All of the texts are out of copyright at this point, but the Bitters did an excellent job organizing and cross-referencing the content. The woman making the pitch said they got it all off of Earth's original world-wide network before it was replaced."

"I met the son of the woman making the presentation," Julie said, omitting Zick's comment about the price. "Sorry to rush off, but I'm supposed to go to my first Drazen martial arts lesson today."

"See you tomorrow morning."

Julie exited the library and went directly to the closest lift tube. The doors snapped opened and she found herself face-to-face with Bill. "How did you get there?"

"I just got off work at the smithy. You're on your way to the dojo, right?"

"Jorb said noon on our clock."

"I've been waiting like five minutes in the lift tube capsule. Flower said it was a technical issue."

"Do you know what deck the dojo's on?"

"No. Flower?" he whispered.

"Are you trying to subvoc?" Julie asked. "I can hear you and you're moving your lips."

"Some of us haven't had an implant as long as others. Flower?" Bill repeated out loud.

"The dojo is located on this deck. I'm not a Stryx station and I don't have that many horizontal crossovers available for lift tubes," the Dollnick AI complained as the capsule set off. "If you weren't so late, I would have suggested jogging there."

"How long would that take?"

"Fifteen minutes if you were in better shape. Tell Jorb you'd like to start a little later and jog there from work. You can swing by the library and pick up Julie on the way. While your theatre practice counts as a team sport, it wouldn't hurt either of you to get some regular aerobic exercise."

"Yes, Flower," they chorused sarcastically, and then grinned at each other.

"I saw that in my thermal imaging, your teeth show up cold. And set aside some time this evening to go over our strategy for the next stop, Bill. It seems I may have made a minor error with the shipment from Bits."

"All of those cash-on-delivery packages?" he asked. "Jorb and Dewey both thought it was odd."

"My basic business concept remains sound, I just need to fine-tune." The doors slid open and Bill followed Julie out into an area of the deck that neither of them had ever visited. "Go right, it's about a minute's walk—less if you were in better shape."

"Are you looking forward to this?" Julie asked Bill.

"As long as he doesn't make us fight each other. He was really good as a fencing teacher."

"The bunny wasn't bad either."

"Listen. I'm sorry about getting sick on your sneakers. I guess I don't have a stomach for rides."

"I forgot about that already," Julie told him. "Don't worry, we're still friends."

"But I want to be—"

"Late," Jorb called from the doorway of the dojo. "I'm not one of those old-fashioned teachers who's going to make you do a hundred tentacle pull-ups, but don't let it become a habit."

"Sorry," Julie said. "I shouldn't have agreed to noon since that's when I get off work at the library."

"Flower suggested that we push the time back a quarter-hour. Come in and get out of your work clothes so we can get started."

"You have uniforms for us?" Bill asked.

"For beginners? Just strip down to your undergarments. The important thing is that your clothes don't impede your movements."

"Not going to happen," Julie declared, but Jorb had already disappeared back through the door. "I don't think he heard me."

"I'll explain it to him," Bill said, and entering the dojo before the girl, he caught up with the Drazen and began talking in an undertone.

"Really?" Jorb asked at his usual volume. "You don't think you can control your animal passions for an hour?"

"That's not what I said," Bill sputtered, his face turning red.

"Just kidding, but I can't start formal lessons while you both look like you're dressed for mining ore."

"They're just blue jeans," Julie said. "We wear them all the time."

"Do they make a shorter version?" the Drazen asked dubiously.

"Shorts. What do your other students usually wear?"

"Well, the girls in the finishing school wear the Vergallian exercise skirts that the headmistress supplies them, but Drazens generally wear fighting trunks and a smock, while the Grenouthians and Verlocks spar naked. Maybe I have a smock you can wear, Bill."

"Are you okay?" Julie asked their teacher, who let out a groan when he bent to check the contents of a chest.

"Graduation exercises this morning," Jorb said. "Thirty-two teenage girls flipped me to show their proficiency, and some of them didn't quite pull back enough on their disabling blows to the throat. It's a good thing I was wearing padding."

"Now I understand why you want to find other work."

"They only graduate four classes a year so the tests aren't a big deal," the Drazen said, straightening up with a grimace and tossing Julie a soccer ball. "I shouldn't complain. Repetition is the key to repeatability and I get paid to practice falling. Sorry, Bill. I thought I had some extra smocks but they must be back in my cabin. Today we'll

93

just work on assessing your general condition so I can design a lesson plan."

"You want us to play soccer?" Julie asked.

"Just put the ball on the floor and stand on it on one foot. I want to check your balance."

"There's no way I can stand on that ball."

"Sure you can. Just do it quickly and don't think about it."

"That's impossible," Julie said, kicking the ball back to the Drazen. "You do it."

Jorb shrugged and then hopped up on the ball, keeping his left leg held out in the air in front of the right. With his arms spread wide and his tentacle sticking out behind him, he executed a series of hops, each time rotating ninety degrees before completing a full revolution. Then he drew his left leg across his body with the knee bent and leaned forward to put his right elbow on his left ankle as if he were sitting in a chair.

"That's amazing," Bill said after several seconds passed during which the Drazen barely twitched. "How long have you been practicing?"

"Since I bought this ball for my required team sport and none of the Humans ever passed to me. It's a lot easier than balancing on a ball without any seams. Try it."

Jorb hopped off the ball, which did a little bounce when relieved of his mass, and kicked it to Bill, who amazed himself by trapping it under his foot. But standing up on the ball didn't go as smoothly, and if Julie hadn't gotten an arm under his shoulder as he flipped off backwards, he might have landed on his head.

"Good spotting," Jorb complimented the girl. "You've got quick reactions for a Human."

"Is there something else we can work on today?" she asked. "I don't have to try standing on a ball to know that I can't."

Eight

"Are you coming along to keep an eye on your camera?" Irene asked the Grenouthian theatre director when he boarded the shuttle. "I haven't run it into anything since that first time you showed me how to guide it, and that was only because you were making me nervous."

"I know you're taking care of the camera because it provides extensive data logging," the bunny replied. He settled his bulk into the open spot next to Irene with a sigh of satisfaction. "I'm not generally a big fan of Dollnick ergonomics but they do a nice job on shuttle seats."

"Speak for yourself," Harry said from the seat on his wife's other side. "Our feet don't reach the deck."

"Then I would suggest folding out the footrest," the director said, bending over and reaching under Irene's seat. A padded footrest swung up and supported her legs at the perfect height.

"Are you serious?" Harry demanded, looking at the ceiling. "When were you going to tell us, Flower?"

"I didn't want to offend you," the AI replied. "The footrests are for Dollnick children."

Around the shuttle, the members of the independent living cooperative, their numbers boosted by ten new additions from Bits, helped each other extend the footrests. Jack stood up at the front of the passenger cabin and did a quick visual count.

"Looks like everybody," he said. "New members, don't forget to take a tracking bracelet from Nancy when we dock."

"What happened to Julie?" somebody asked.

"She's getting overtime at the library this stop," Nancy replied. "Flower is expecting over a hundred thousand visitors during the three days we're here."

"Which brings up my next point," Jack continued. "Timble is one of the most visited orbitals in this sector, thanks to the high level of interest in documentaries and dramas produced here. Expect to see a lot of aliens, not counting the Grenouthians, of course."

"Of course," the director echoed ironically.

"Since when do the Grenouthians produce dramas?" Dave asked him. "I thought it was all documentaries and news."

"Our dramas are too refined for the average sentient. They are produced primarily for our domestic market, though I understand they're also popular with the Cayl and some of the other alpha-species."

"So remember the two B's," Jack said, holding up two fingers. "Bracelet," he folded down a finger, "Buddy system," he folded down the second. "Flower informs me that we'll be docking at the orbital in less than ten minutes, so try not to fall asleep."

"I wonder why Flower doesn't just extend an airlock to the orbital so we could walk over without taking the shuttle," Harry said to his wife.

"A small matter of spinning on her axis," the bunny answered from Irene's other side. "It's possible for two spinning structures to connect in space, but it's generally not worth the aggravation. Timble has at least three times

Flower's capacity, but it's not big enough to fit her in a docking bay."

"Is Timble self-aware?" Irene asked.

"It's just a large orbital with lots of residential decks, studio space, and a theme park under construction. I haven't been here since almost fifty years ago when we made a stop during one of my regional theatre tours."

"You used to direct regional theatre?" Harry asked.

"I was an actor," the bunny replied. "An actor, and a ticket taker, and a bartender, and a tent raiser. You do it all when you play on the road."

"And what are we going to do if you take this job?" Irene asked. "I read your script for the play about making documentaries and I was looking forward to dressing up as an alien."

"I'll have to find a replacement for myself. I never thought I would regret leaving Flower, but I originally came aboard to build a studio and train Humans in developing your own programming. Then our host declared theatre a team sport, and the resulting demand kept me too busy to complete my original goal."

"So that's why you have all the camera equipment," Irene said. "I wondered when you took me to the storage area."

"The room you are referring to as a storage area was intended to be an immersive studio."

"And that's why you joined Flower?" Irene asked.

"The Open University held a competition on Union Station to award funding and Stryx backing for new business ventures. Their hope was that alien entrepreneurs would act as force multipliers in Flower's mission of knitting together your sovereign communities before you all go native."

"I didn't know that," Harry said. "I thought everybody was just trying to make a living."

"Everybody everywhere is trying to make a living, but that's not enough of a reason to take up residence on a colony ship that keeps going around in circles visiting Human population centers. In my pitch to the committee on Union Station, I pointed out that Humans have barely above zero percent of the entertainment market because you're all so busy watching immersives from other species that you aren't developing your own shows. I proposed constructing a studio on Flower to give the locals a chance to have their holo presence evaluated, and I offered to direct theatre as a bonus."

"I thought you liked directing plays," Irene said.

"Can you guess how old I am?" the Grenouthian asked suddenly.

Harry and his wife looked at each other and decided that it was safest to let the question pass.

"Four hundred and eleven in your years. I'm in the prime of life and I haven't earned a Production Guild card yet. It's humiliating."

"What did you do before working in regional theatre?"

"I spent a few centuries in the family trading business but I knew I'd never be happy. I put off marriage to start over again in the entertainment industry."

"So this is really a big deal for you, being invited to direct documentaries."

"Almost too good to be true. My family removed me from the rolls for bringing dishonor on them by rejecting our ancestral business. If I can make a name for myself in entertainment, all will be forgiven. I haven't been home in over sixty years."

"Then we wish you the best of luck," Harry said sincerely. "Break a leg, or whatever Grenouthians say."

"Hop to it," the bunny informed him.

"Attention," Flower announced. "I will be docking the shuttle in thirty seconds. Please return your footrests to the stored position when you get up so nobody will trip over them. The spin rate of the deck where I'll be parking the shuttle will give you a weight of approximately ninety percent of Earth normal. Thank you for choosing Flower's Transportation Services and have a nice day."

The shuttle seats, which had rotated one hundred and eighty degrees mid-trip to keep the passengers from pulling against their safety restraints when the acceleration away from Flower had flipped to deceleration towards Timble, returned to their forward-facing orientation. The weight of the occupants increased steadily as the Dollnick AI matched the shuttle's velocity to the spinning orbital, and only the gentlest of lurches witnessed that the docking sequence was complete.

"I have to admit that she does that well," the Grenouthian said, rising to his furry feet and grabbing his portfolio. "Try not to interfere with any productions while you're nosing around."

"Hop to it," Harry called after the bunny, who reached the hatch just as it opened. "I'll fold in your footrest, Irene. You take care of the camera."

The members of the independent living cooperative filed out past Nancy and Jack, receiving a tracking bracelet from the former and a small stack of flyers from the latter.

"Are these even necessary anymore?" one man inquired on receiving the flyers. "Flower's advertising has to be reaching a million times more people."

"Advertising is passive," Dave said, accepting his own stack of flyers. "I was in sales all of my life and there's nothing easier to ignore than a commercial. Next comes a piece of mail, and after that a video call, but if you're serious about selling, you have to show up in person."

"And deliver a piece of mail," the other man grumbled.

"What treatment is the Farling doctor pushing this stop?" Harry asked Dave, as he followed his fellow board member along the marked path on the deck.

"Special on cosmetic dental work," the former salesman said. "He offered to redo my crowns for free if I send him three customers."

"Is there something wrong with your crowns?"

"Not yet, but I'm banking my commission. I had them done on Earth and you know they don't last forever."

"Where are we going?" Irene asked, motioning the floating camera through a slow rotation to capture the entire docking bay. "It seems like a long walk."

"I think we're all just following the director," Dave said. "I saw him disappear through the revolving doors up there right after I left the shuttle."

"Who builds with revolving doors in space? I haven't seen any since Harry and I spent our honeymoon in New York City."

"Probably a backup for the atmosphere retention field," Jack answered from behind her. "The docking bay shares the same atmosphere as the orbital, but the revolving door will lock closed if there's a failure."

"Why not a sliding door?" Harry asked.

"If the atmosphere retention field failed, a sliding door could get stuck open if somebody collapsed on the threshold. The thing about revolving doors is that they're always closed to airflow, no matter where they stop moving. I

101

wouldn't be surprised if they used them in busy buildings on Earth to limit heating and air-conditioning losses."

By the time Jack finished his explanation they reached the revolving doors. Irene hesitated for a moment, then gestured the floating camera in close to her body where she could grab it if necessary. Dave followed a couple of the new members through, then Harry and Irene entered, leaving Jack and Nancy to bring up the rear.

"Are we in line?" Dave asked when their progress came to a sudden halt.

"The woman in front of me said that we're at customs."

"Is Jack here yet?" somebody called from the front.

"On my way," the president of the cooperative shouted back, before adding under his breath to Nancy, "I told you there would be bribery involved."

The group split like the Red Sea to allow their champion to move to the front of the line, where a large bunny wearing a black silk sash was impatiently tapping his foot.

"Papers," the customs agent demanded.

"I think my ear cuff translation device must be malfunctioning. Your species stopped using paper millions of years ago."

"We reintroduced it on this orbital to make our Human guest workers feel at home," the Grenouthian replied. "I assume you have filled out a Form 227.0031?"

Jack made a show of patting down his pockets before saying, "I must have left it on my dresser."

"Normally I'd suggest having your group wait while you go back and fetch it, but there are several large shuttles inbound from Flower and there's no room for standing around, as you can see. What to do..." The customs agent combed the fur under his chin in thought, four stubby fingers each leaving a line in the downy white.

"If I know Flower, she's already pulled back our shuttle," Jack said, scratching his temple with his index finger. "I know it's not your problem, but another round trip would break our budget."

"What are there? Forty-six of you?" The Grenouthian did a quick count, using two fingers held together as a pointer.

"You know we're not very good at math. Could we round that to fifty?"

"You mean cash?" the bunny asked in an undertone.

"Thank you for your understanding in this matter," Jack said. He offered the customs agent a handshake, during which the unmistakable sound of clinking coins could be heard.

"Enjoy your visit. Move along."

As Harry and Irene passed the desk, the customs agent popped back up and asked, "Who are you with?"

"Flower's Paradise," Harry replied.

"Is that a new production company?"

"It's our independent living community on Flower. We're all retired, sort of."

"Where did you get the broadcast-quality camera?"

"Oh," Irene said. "It belongs to the director of our theatre group. He would have come through right before us."

"Unbelievable," the bunny muttered, moving aside. "That camera is worth more than three cycles of my salary and he lets a Human play with it."

"Do you think he was serious about the cost?" Irene asked her husband nervously. "I knew it wasn't cheap, but isn't three cycles almost a half a year?"

"I heard about these custom guys working in the alien cafeteria," Harry said. "Their salary is just for bookkeeping, they make their money on bribes."

"Why would an advanced species stand for that?"

"Tradition? Efficiency? Nepotism? Maybe Flower could tell us."

"Any problems?" Jack asked. "When you didn't come out, I was worried he was trying to hold you up for another payment."

"He was just curious about the camera," Irene said. "How did you negotiate that bribe?"

"Practice. There was none of that nonsense on Dollnick worlds, but I visited enough places during my brief stint as a trader to learn how to grease palms. The funny thing is that I thought we were bargaining for the whole group in increments of a hundred and it turned out that the bunny was charging per head. In the end, I paid half of what I planned and was able to tip."

"You tip people who bribe you?" Harry asked incredulously.

"It's always a good idea to tip aliens so that dealing with our species doesn't leave a bad taste in their mouths. Think of it like arctic explorers leaving caches of supplies they may never need."

"Where did everybody go?" Irene asked as they emerged into a cavernous hall. Giant display panels showing productions in progress covered the walls.

"We're all going to meet back here in three hours and we'll find somewhere to eat together," Nancy said. "I already talked to a woman who told me that the studios have observer galleries with audio suppression fields where we can watch a production or try approaching potential members."

"How will we find our way back here?" Harry asked.

"Look up," Nancy said, pointing at the display over the corridor they had just come from.

104

"It's Flower," Irene said, recognizing the giant image of the Dollnick colony ship they called home. "So as long as we get back to this central hall we'll be set. Is this the only public access area on the orbital?"

"No, but the woman I spoke with said it's the one with the most studios attached. The new theme park for Earth documentaries is on the other end of the orbital, but it's still under construction, so it's off-limits to visitors."

"Irene and I will just hand out some flyers, have a look around, and see you all back here in three hours," Harry said, itching to get started. Twenty minutes later, his enthusiasm had dulled. "What am I doing wrong?" he asked his wife. "I've never had such a bad response before."

"You mean from all three times you've handed out flyers," she teased him.

"They keep asking me what programs are produced on board Flower. It's like they're all addicted to immersives."

"I suppose it is pretty exciting here with all of the people milling around. You can feel the energy, and apparently there's plenty of work because people are still coming in from Earth."

"But what kind of—excuse me," Harry interrupted himself to offer a flyer to an older man who had paused to look at one of the large displays. "I'm here from the independent living cooperative on Flower and we're looking for new members."

The man offered Harry a maniacal grin and then began tugging at the skin on his face, which stretched out like a cartoon character. Then the whole mask came away with a popping sound, and a man in his mid-twenties was revealed.

"Sorry, Grandpa," he said. "I was just on set."

"Wait a second," Irene called after the actor as he began to walk away. "Aren't there enough older actors here to play senior roles?"

"It's not that simple," the young man explained. "The Grenouthians have rules about the number of hours we can work, and age plays into it. By the time you're seventy, unless you have a twin you can share a role with, the opportunities start disappearing. They're going to enforce even tighter restrictions for the theme park because it's considered live theatre."

"I'd heard of something like that for babies, but—"

"Why would babies need breaks?" the actor interrupted. "They don't have any lines, and all they do is sleep. Anyway, if you're looking for retired actors, they mainly hang around the cafes at that end of the hall," he concluded, pointing in one direction and heading off the opposite way.

"Did you get all that on camera?" Harry asked his wife.

"Yes, but I don't think we could use it without permission."

"I think Flower follows her own rules about privacy. I'm starting to feel like a kid without a prom date, so let's go try those cafes."

When Harry and Irene arrived in an area set up like an Italian piazza with hundreds of small tables surrounded by coffee shops, they weren't surprised to find that the rest of the visitors from Flower's Paradise were already mining this vein of geriatric gold.

"Yes, I saw your story in the Galactic Free Press, and I've also seen the ads you've been running here," an elderly lady told Harry. "Are you paid per head for bringing in prospects?"

106

"We don't even keep count, though maybe we should start. The truth is, we have a deadline to get our membership up to a hundred to justify keeping our section of the eighty-percent-gravity deck open, though since the newspaper article came out, it looks like we'll make that easy. But spreading the word gives us something to do on these outings other than walking around and gaping like tourists."

"I like that," the woman said. "I'm feeling kind of useless myself since the Grenouthians cut my work limit down to four and a half hours a day, and that includes putting on makeup, mind you. In addition to limiting the parts I can try out for to 'Old woman #3 in the crowd' it means I can never work enough hours to earn golden time."

"If you don't mind my asking, do you need the money?"

"Not as long as the Grenouthians remain solvent. I opted for the defined benefits pension plan almost forty years ago when I first started acting in their documentaries. I could have retired after two decades based on my life expectancy. It's just hard to let go."

"It might be easier if you weren't living in a giant studio," Harry said. "We're having an open house tomorrow, the details are all on the flyer."

"You're offering me a special on cosmetic dental surgery?"

"Sorry, I always do that. Turn it over."

"I'll give it some thought. My name is Ophelia, by the way. Is that your wife with the camera?"

"Irene."

"Pity. The good ones are always taken."

Nine

"Mr. Duck?" Bill asked hopefully.

"Donald. Are you an agent?"

"No, I'm with Next Stop Deliveries. I have your Game Master."

"My handheld? I'd given up on ever seeing it again. I must have brought it in to the local repair guy two years ago and he had to send it out. Thanks."

"The price is on the tag. Cool name, by the way."

"I changed it five years ago so casting directors would notice me," Donald said, accepting the package. "The repair guy told me it would be around—WHAT!"

"I can only accept cash."

Donald thrust the package back into Bill's hands. "That's five times what I paid to buy it at the vintage games store."

"According to the slip, they replaced the screen, the processor, and the keypad, so basically it's new. Does anybody even sell these anymore?"

"I don't know. I only got it for when I was waiting in line at casting calls, but now I go over the scripts instead and I'm getting more parts."

"Oh. So you don't want it?"

"I'm not going to pay seventy creds for an obsolete hand-held game. In fact, I'm pretty sure I've seen a

Dollnick knockoff that plays every old Earth game ever published for a quarter of the cost of the repair."

"I apologize for wasting your time," Bill said, putting the package back into his shoulder duffle and turning away.

"Where are you going?"

"I've got sixteen more deliveries to make. Sorry if I interrupted you."

"Hold on there a minute. Did I say I didn't want it? I'm just not paying seventy creds."

"But the tag—"

"How long have you had this job?" Donald interrupted.

"About a week, though you're actually my first delivery."

"And what do you think your employers are going to do with the package if you take it back?"

"I don't know. Maybe we'll have an auction or something? And I'm not an employee, I'm a partner."

"If you're ownership, it means you have room to negotiate these things."

"I'm not so sure."

"I'd go five creds."

"Let me check with my partner," Bill said. "I've got a new implant but I'm not sure it will reach. Without even trying to subvoc, he ventured, "Flower?"

"Have you gotten in trouble already?" the Dollnick AI responded in his head.

"I'm with Mr. Duck and he doesn't want to pay the seventy creds."

"How much is he offering?"

"Five."

There was a brief pause, and then Flower said, "Ask for ten and don't settle for less than seven."

"Uh, I have to ask for ten," Bill said.

"The games aren't even that interesting," Donald countered. "Maybe I could go five and a half since you came all the way out here."

"I can't go under seven."

"Six."

"I wasn't bargaining. I mean I really can't go under seven or my partner will make me run laps around the reservoir deck or something."

"I forgot that you're new at this," Donald said. "I'll tell you what. Normally I'd tip for delivery, but my dad always told me not to tip the owner, so instead of adding a cred for you, I'll pay the seven. But next time somebody wants to haggle, don't try jumping to your bottom line price so fast."

"Thanks," Bill said, accepting the coins and handing the package over. "I hope it works."

"What? Hey, wait a second. I want to turn it on," Donald said, tearing off the packaging. He hit the power button and the screen of the device lit up with a menu and played a simple tune. Then his thumbs began tapping on the controls, and after a minute, Bill gave up on getting his attention and left.

"Well? What happened?" Flower demanded in Bill's head as he headed for the next address on the list.

"He went for it. I thought you could hear whatever I hear, like with Julie."

"Not unless you give me permission."

"Let me think about it. Is ten percent of the amount on the tag our new target price?"

"Didn't you say you worked with your mother as a street vendor when you were a child?"

110

"We didn't have to bargain much because our prices were already way below market."

"If you collect ten percent for all of the packages I'll break even on the upfront payment I made in apples. But that doesn't account for our expenses, so get whatever you can."

"I don't want to overcharge people."

"The galaxy is built on mercantilism. You're in business now, so deal with it."

Six hours later, Bill tracked down the last addressee in the ready room for background actors at the studio where her brother said she was working. By this time, he had figured out that if he asked for twenty percent of the cash-on-delivery amount, he didn't feel like he was trying to rob people, and they quickly came to an agreement. The girl, who was a year or two younger than himself, was so pleased to get her hand-held game back while collecting double-time to wait around during a production snag that she paid the asking price without question.

"That's it, Flower," Bill whispered as he headed back for the main hall. "Jason Levine refused his package, said that he had broken the addiction and he didn't want it back at any price, and Bethany Harrel no longer lives on Timble and nobody could tell me where she went. I think we did okay."

"Good timing, I was about to ping you. Dewey could use some help loading."

"Why is he here?"

"Picking up. Ask a lift tube to take you to Industrial Zone Six."

"Got it," Bill said, and turned around as he had just passed a lift tube. He had to wait a minute for a capsule to arrive, and then he requested, "Industrial Zone Six."

"Warning," the lift tube informed him. "You have requested an active industrial area which could be hazardous to your health. Do you wish to continue?"

"I guess," Bill said.

"Do you wish to continue?"

"Yes," he affirmed, realizing that the software controlling the lift tubes was looking for legal consent rather than a conversation. The trip took almost ten minutes, the longest he'd ever spent in a lift tube, and when the doors finally slid open, he was glad that Flower had insisted he wear magnetic cleats. Bill clicked his heels to activate the magnets before shuffling out of the capsule.

A fork truck which reminded him of logging equipment he'd seen in a documentary about Earth almost ran him down. Bill jumped back against the now-closed doors of the lift tube as it shot passed, the Grenouthian driver cursing fluently.

"I'm here, Flower," he said out loud, too flustered to try to subvoc. "Which way now?"

"Your signal is approximately four hundred meters from Dewey's current location. Without full access to your implant, I can't guarantee your safe arrival."

"All right already, do what you want."

"That's how partnerships should work," Flower said smugly. "Stay to your right and try not to get run over by any cargo handling equipment."

"What's Dewey doing down here anyway?" Bill asked, breaking into a shuffling jog to get out of the heavily trafficked area as quickly as possible. "Are the Grenouthians hiring you to make a delivery?"

"It's more of a consignment, and I've already got it sold to vendors in the bazaar. How much cash do you have?"

"Just under two hundred creds, I think. I lost count when it passed my monthly pay for helping Harry part-time in the cafeteria."

"Excellent, that should be enough to close the add-on deal."

"Don't I have to bring it back? I thought you were going to teach me how to keep books."

"I am. Rule number one is not to write anything down if you don't have to. Rule number two is that money is only working when it's changing hands. Be ready to turn left."

Bill looked back over his shoulder and skidded to a halt as a number of cargo containers floating about knee-high off the deck barreled past in a chain. Then he looked the other way, back again, and shuffled rapidly across the travel lane. As he continued along the new route, he couldn't help noticing that the lighting was getting dimmer.

"Are you sure this is the right direction?" he asked after another minute. "I can barely see my feet."

"You shouldn't be looking at your feet, you should be watching for Dewey's signal."

"But I can't see far enough to—is that him?"

"Do you see a blinking red light moving back and forth in a straight line?"

"Yes. On my way." Bill moved forward as fast as he could, and as he grew closer to the assistant librarian, he saw that the lights were actually stationary LEDs embedded in Dewey's shelving attachment that gave the illusion of movement by blinking on and off in sequence. Then a dim hulk moved across the way between them and Bill halted again.

"What are you doing?" Flower asked.

"Something just crossed between us. It was big."

"Like the Grenouthian we're doing business with?"

"Oh, right. He moved on."

"He'll be back. Dewey just approved the sample and the Grenouthian is retrieving the shipment now."

Bill moved forward cautiously, coming to a halt at a distance where he could reach out and touch the assistant librarian's shelving attachment.

"The Grenouthian will be back in a minute," Dewey said in a whisper.

"Why are you whispering?" Bill asked in a muted tone.

"It can be tricky doing business with warehouse workers. We don't want to end up having to make deals with all of them."

"Do they all have consignments?"

"Is that what Flower called it? Shhh. Here he comes."

Bill's eyes had finally adjusted to the point that he could make out a burly bunny pulling some sort of floating platform piled high with crates. Having learned his lesson about the momentum of large masses in low gravity, Bill moved out of the way, and the Grenouthian expertly brought the cargo to a halt just a few steps from the airlock.

"Do you have the extras we were discussing?" Dewey asked.

"I've got them, but they'll cost you five hundred cash – no more fruit," the alien grunted.

"My associates are willing to pay fifty."

"I'd give these to my offspring for their sticker collections before I'd sell that low. Four hundred."

"You understand that we can just manufacture our own, and we're already paying top cred for the merchandise."

"I gave you the volume discount. Three hundred is my absolute minimum."

"I could see going a hundred, but that's just for future consideration."

"Two hundred or you can forget about doing business with me in the future."

"My partner will give you the money," Dewey said.

"I haven't counted it yet," Bill said, bringing a fistful of creds out of his pocket. "I can't even see in here well enough to—"

"Just give it here," the Grenouthian interrupted impatiently, holding out his cupped hands. Bill carefully poured the creds onto the hairy palms, and the bunny gave a grunt of satisfaction. "I'll keep the extra eight creds as a tip for helping you load. Let's get a move on before somebody comes."

The airlock hissed open, and Dewey immediately began loading his shelving attachment with crates. "Help me, Bill, and then grab a couple of boxes yourself."

Between the three of them, they cleared off half of the floater in one trip, and then returned for the rest, barely leaving enough room for themselves in the airlock.

"And the extras?" Dewey demanded.

"In here," the bunny said, prying up the lid of the one crate that was smaller than all of the others. Bill thought he saw something change position as he looked in, but the assistant librarian was satisfied.

"Flower sends her regards. Let's do this again our next time through."

"Off you go," the Grenouthian said, stepping back and hitting the airlock button. Through the small window, Bill saw the lights come back on full in the warehouse section they'd just vacated.

The outer airlock opened on the familiar interior of the bookmobile, and they rapidly transferred the crates. Dewey carried the special box up front to the pilot's seat. "Coming, Bill?"

"Right behind you. How do I disconnect the docking arm."

"Just close our hatch and it disengages automatically."

As soon as he hit the button, Bill felt his weight disappear entirely, and the only thing keeping his feet in place were the magnetic cleats. "What happened?"

"As soon as the docking arm freed us, our angular acceleration fell to zero, like releasing a rock from a sling," Dewey said. "Look out the viewport."

Bill pressed his nose against the crystal and saw the decks of the spinning orbital blurring past.

"Wow! How did you ever dock with that thing in the first place?"

"I'm a pretty good pilot, but I let Flower handle the fancy vector stuff. The docking arms are always on the flat ends of cylindrical structures, and you need pretty fine control to match velocity with an airlock that's moving in a circle. It's actually easier to enter a docking bay and let the manipulator fields damp any differentials."

"The bunny couldn't have moved our merchandise to a docking bay?"

"The docking bays have customs inspectors who add another layer of expenses."

"How did you get so good at negotiating, Dewey?"

"I've been collecting overdue library books for years. If I held out for the calculated fine, I'd never get the money or the books."

"So what were those 'extras' I paid for?"

"Come up here and take a look."

Bill carefully moved forward, planting one magnet-cleated boot after the other, and grabbed the back of the co-pilot's chair. As soon as he was seated with the four-point safety harness in place, Dewey passed him the box.

"Holographic stickers of a bunny with a camera?" Bill asked after peering inside.

"If you change your viewing angle, the camera moves."

"I think I've seen these before but I can't remember where."

"I guess you were never a big documentary fan," Dewey said. "They're authenticity stickers for entertainment-system-compatible memory modules. That's what we loaded back there."

"What does Flower want with a bunch of blank memory modules?"

"They aren't blank," the assistant librarian said, and the aperture on one of his binocular lenses dialed down to a pinpoint before snapping open again in his version of a lidless wink.

"We're going into the video pirating business?"

"I think you're missing the point here," Flower said in his head. "What's that on your lap?"

"A box of fake authenticity holograms."

"If I wanted fake authenticity holograms I'd manufacture them myself. We just paid two-hundred and eight creds for those."

"I don't get it."

"What's the difference between an authorized copy of a documentary and an unauthorized copy?"

"I guess if it's authorized, that means you pay the Grenouthians for it."

"And who did we just buy these from?"

"I meant the real producers, not some bunny in a warehouse who turned down the lights so nobody could see what he was doing," Bill protested.

"Now you're splitting hairs," Flower said. "The Grenouthian with the entertainment booth at the bazaar commissioned us to pick up a shipment of documentaries from a Grenouthian on Timble, and we're throwing in a whole box of Grenouthian-made holographic authenticity stickers. What could be more kosher than that?"

"Prepare for acceleration," Dewey announced. "I'm about to engage the engine."

"I thought Flower was piloting," Bill said.

"Only the docking sequence. I've let us drift away from the orbital in case anybody was watching, but we're in the clear now." A soft humming sound began and Bill was pressed back in his seat, almost biting his tongue as he had been about to ask another question.

"I've been rethinking the whole delivery concept, and I've decided we might do better with a concierge service," Flower continued over Bill's implant.

"What does that mean?"

"Less work for more money and better tips."

"I meant the word."

"It's the closest term I could find in your limited language to describe someone who provides a high level of service that includes handling packages without asking too many questions."

"Smuggling?"

"Where do you get these ideas? Smuggling is illegal."

"And what we're doing is legal?" Bill asked sharply.

"It's a grey area. Don't you trust me to do what's best for you?"

"I let you start listening in on my implant, didn't I?"

118

"Oooh, bad move," Dewey muttered.

"But why would you encourage piracy?" Bill asked. "You're going into production yourself."

"I want to learn about the distribution side of the entertainment business and it makes sense to start locally. I intend to cultivate a relationship with the Grenouthians who sell dramas and documentaries in the bazaar. When my own animated production is ready, I hope they'll be willing to use their contacts to help me distribute it throughout our circuit and beyond."

"I don't understand. How will having access to piracy networks help? Razood told me that pirates sell cheap because they aren't paying anything to the producer."

"It's called guerilla marketing," the Dollnick AI explained patiently. "The galactic entertainment business is extremely crowded, and just getting attention for new productions requires an enormous amount of ad spend. I've been running the numbers for a launch promotion, and it turns out that for many audiences, including Humans, it's cheaper to build an audience by giving away content than by selling it through advertising."

"But you won't make any money," Bill pointed out.

"Look at it this way," Flower said. "Let's say I create an animated feature that I could sell into the home entertainment market for three creds a viewer, ignoring the cost of delivery media. If I have to spend four creds on advertising to make each sale, my profit is actually higher if I simply hand the master over to the pirates and let them bear the copying and distribution costs."

"What profit?"

"It's all in the bookkeeping."

Ten

"A hamburger deluxe with steak fries, hold the pickle," Julie called over the counter to the cook.

Without even turning his head, Hank sang back,

Hold the burger, hold the bun
Human diets are no fun
Eat like that, you'll lose a ton
Human Burger

"Did you just make that up?"

"I heard it at the open house that Human Burger ran here looking for new employees a few months ago. If you work at one of their outlets in Drazen space, you have to be able to make up songs for the customers."

"You were thinking of quitting your family's diner and taking a job with Human Burger?"

"I was just curious, though the education benefits were terrific. They're owned by Eccentric Enterprises, the same outfit that Flower supposedly works for, though everybody knows that it's just a front for EarthCent Intelligence."

"I didn't know."

"Well, you're new. Anyway, I thought I'd try to get you motivated for your singing lesson."

"So this is where it all happens," a new voice announced, and Julie turned to see Zick taking a seat next to the waitress station. "Can I get a coffee?"

"You look tired," Julie observed, reaching over the counter for the pot and mug, and then pouring a cup for him. "Cream or sugar?"

"Black, like my heart."

"What's that supposed to mean?"

"It's just a pirate saying," Zick reassured her. "I've been up for thirty-six hours working on a char for Flower's competition. Wanna see it?"

"Uh, sure. What's a char?"

"It's short for a character," Zick explained. He unfolded his tab and brought up an image of a bulky alien with leathery skin and three-toed feet. "Flower wanted new ideas for alien superheroes so I came up with a Verlock ninja. I call him Slomo, for slow motion."

"What does he do?"

"Everything a ninja should do, but slower. Here, watch his roundhouse kick."

The alien character executed a flawless martial arts move that would have knocked the head off an opponent who somehow failed to see it coming. Given that the Verlock moved like he was submerged in molasses, surprise seemed unlikely.

"But what's the point of a ninja who can't fight?" Julie asked.

"He can fight, just slowly," Zick pointed out. "Anyway, the competition is for chars, not stories, though I do all three."

"Chars and stories only makes two."

"I code too. I'm a triple threat."

121

"So if you were coming up with a story, what would you do with your slow ninja?" Julie asked. Against her will, she found herself drawn in by the bizarre animation of a fighter from the advanced species that was known primarily for its mathematical and scientific acumen.

"I'd find a way to make him effective," Zick answered without hesitation. "Like, there could be an enemy with a kinetic suppression field that restricts everybody to slow motion, and Slomo would be the only fighter who wasn't thrown off his game. Or maybe he can drink a potion and move at normal speed for a while. Potions are always good for storylines in games because then you have to manage your inventory and search for more."

"He's actually kind of cool," Julie said, taking the two plates that Hank gave her, and balancing one on her forearm to keep a hand free for the ketchup bottle. "I never did anything creative like that." Then she brought the food out to the couple at table five and returned again to the counter.

"Do you want to come to the competition with me?" Zick asked. "They're going to project all of the chars in a giant hologram as Flower chooses the winners. Everybody from Bits is going to be there."

"All twenty thousand of you?"

"Well, the five thousand or so who came up with new chars, though most of them worked in teams. I'm heading there right after I finish this, and maybe one of those chocolate donuts," he added, with a hungry look at the pastry display. "Maybe two."

Julie removed the glass bell lid and used individual waxed papers to pull out two of the chocolate-glazed chocolate donuts. "I have a singing lesson after work."

"You could come later. The competition will be going on for hours."

"This evening is theatre rehearsal, it's my required team sport."

"Okay, I didn't mean to push," Zick said, though he sounded disappointed. "How long have you been singing?"

"I haven't, I mean, this is my first lesson. I only signed up because the Drazen who runs the dojo suggested it."

"You train in martial arts with an alien? I've seen the Drazens in professional cage fights. Their tentacles make it impossible for humans to compete with them."

"Jorb promised to keep it behind his back. He mentioned that it's hard to find humans willing to sign up for his classes because of the tentacle."

"I know some people who might be interested," Zick said. "How do I contact him?"

"Just ask Flower for Jorb's dojo."

"Hey, Julie," said a pretty girl whose hair was arranged on a trellis in imitation of the Frunge style. "If you have somewhere to go, you don't have to wait for the end of your shift."

"Thanks, Renée," Julie responded. "I'm going to my first singing lesson so I'd like to get there early."

"Who's this handsome guy you're plying with donuts?"

"Oh, this is Zick, he just joined Flower at Bits. Zick, Renée," she introduced them formally.

"Wanna see my char?" Zick asked immediately.

"Sure, I love anime," Renée replied. "I heard there's going to be a big competition tonight and I'm planning on stopping in if it's still going when I get off work. I'm only on for the dinner rush."

Julie took her leave and headed for the nearest lift tube, where she instructed the capsule, "Choral Creations, please."

"That Zick has talent, but Bill is better for you," Flower said as the capsule moved off.

"I thought you promised not to get involved in my love life or lack thereof."

"I can play back our verbal contract if you need your memory refreshed, but my part of the agreement was limited to—"

"All right, no need to go all legal on me," Julie interrupted. "I'm nervous about my lesson."

"Why? Because I made fun of your singing in the shower? I think all Humans sound funny."

"What about Drazens?"

"They're very good, actually. They win all of the major tournaments, you know."

"Singing tournaments?"

"The tunnel network species compete at everything, if you haven't noticed," the Dollnick AI said, as the capsule's door slid open on an unfamiliar corridor. "Turn right."

"Thanks. Where am I?"

"The main education deck. I like keeping things organized."

"You don't think I'm overdoing it with the two jobs, the dojo, my theatre practice, and now singing?"

"Idle Humans make work for the social services. Besides, all of your activities could end up tying together."

"How's that?"

"Well, you could get a role performing in a musical with fighting. Now through the doors in front of you," Flower instructed over Julie's implant. "You're a bit early, but so are all of the parents who come to listen to their children, so go right in."

"That's a change from being told I'm not early enough," the girl said. She paused just outside the range of the door's proximity sensor and took a deep breath. "I can't believe I let you and Jorb talk me into this."

"Developing your singing voice will open new career options, in addition to boosting your endorphin and oxytocin levels, which M793qK reported were on the low side."

"And what will that do?"

"Make you feel better," the AI said. "Just go in."

The door slid open on what sounded like a chorus of angels, which almost stopped her in her tracks. She edged through the opening, keeping her back to the wall, and found herself standing with a group of parents, none of whom noticed her arrival.

In the center of the room, a brown-skinned alien with hair almost as long as her tentacle stood with her back to the door. She was conducting a large group of children whose ages ran from as young as six or seven to as old as perhaps twelve. A few of the taller boys might have been borderline tenors, but the rest of the group were definitely altos or sopranos, and they were pouring their hearts into the song about—Julie frowned.

"Flower?" she subvoced. "Are they really singing about radioactive ore extraction techniques?"

"It's a classic Drazen song," the Dollnick AI replied. "Try disabling the translation."

"You mean they aren't singing in English?" Julie flipped the mental switch to turn off the translation function of her implant, and the words of the song were suddenly out of reach, though the musical impact was undiminished.

"How can the implant have kept the tune while translating the meaning?"

"Haven't you noticed that when you're conversing with members of other species the emotional content of their speech comes through clearly? High-end implants aren't limited to merely running a translation. They map the other components of speech and sound to the appropriate areas of your brain."

The Drazen choir mistress let her arms fall to her sides and the concert came to an abrupt end. Released from the spell of the music, the children reverted to their native state and rushed for their parents or the bathroom, depending on their personal needs. A little boy dragged his father over to Julie and introduced her as "The reading circle lady who taught me how to say 'rhinoceros.'"

The man shook her hand and muttered under his breath, "And he's been saying it a hundred times a day ever since."

Finally, the room was empty, and the choir mistress approached Julie with a shy smile. "I'm Rinka, but that's just the English translation for Eldest Daughter. If you've never met any Drazen females, our true names are musical notes that don't translate."

"I'm Julie," the girl replied, accepting the warm handshake. "Do Drazen males also have musical names?"

"We just call them whatever," Rinka said with a giggle. "Most of them can't even read musical notation."

"Is that due to a physical difference between you?"

"They just don't pay attention to their lessons while they're young and it's nearly impossible to learn when you're older. Have you ever sung in a chorus?"

"I'm afraid not," Julie said. "Singing in the shower is about it for me."

"Do you have a favorite song you'd like to perform for me so I can assess your level?"

"How about we just assume it's zero and start from there," Julie suggested. "I suspect that I'm tone-deaf."

"Oh, I doubt that very much. Did you get here in time for the end of the children's practice?"

"It was so beautiful that I almost cried."

"Then you aren't tone-deaf, but let's do a quick test. Did you grow up on Earth?"

"Yes, a place called New York."

"I have the sheet music for a test one of your governments used to administer for free over your pre-Stryx network. Flower found it for me." Rinka led Julie to an upright piano against the wall, and taking her seat on the bench, commented, "Can you believe that I got this instrument for free the last time we stopped at Earth? I had to pay to bring it up on the elevator, but the owner was just happy that it was going to a good home."

"I remember seeing pianos in abandoned apartments when I was a child. They're just too heavy to move."

The Drazen swiped the extra thumb on her left hand across the large tab that sat on the music stand and brought up a series of musical bars with English song titles.

"If this is a test, I just cheated by accident," Julie said. "I couldn't help reading the titles and I recognized most of them."

"That doesn't matter for this test," Rinka said. Then she played through a dozen notes of the first song. "Did that sound right to you?"

"Yes?"

"You don't sound sure."

"I mean, there was a note in the middle that might have been lower than I recall, but then it went back to normal."

"Have you ever heard a song played one note at a time?"

"Probably not," Julie said. "It's different."

"I'm going to play each of these, and if something sounds off to you, just tap my shoulder and I'll go on to the next one."

A few minutes later, Rinka gave her the results. "Twenty-five out of twenty-six, you have fine pitch. Are you ready to try a duet with me?"

"Are you kidding?"

"Something simple. Do you know the theme song to Let's Make Friends?'"

"Everybody knows that one."

"I'll play it through once on the piano first, and the second time we'll sing along." Rinka played through the chords with both hands, though she kept her extra thumbs folded in. Then she launched into the song lyrics and Julie forced herself to join in.

Don't be a stranger, because I look funny.
You look weird to me, but let's make friends.
I'll give you a tissue, if your nose is runny.
I'm as scared as you, so let's make friends.

Julie ran out of breath at the end and broke into a coughing fit.

"Oh, dear," Rinka said. "Perhaps we should start with breathing techniques. Do you often find yourself short of breath when you're talking?"

"I never really noticed, but I don't usually talk all that much."

"Here, let's start with an exercise I do with the children. First, let's stand up, shoulders relaxed, but no slouching," the Drazen said, positioning herself next to Julie. "Look, we're almost exactly the same height."

"Unless you count your tentacle."

"Oh, it goes up by itself sometimes when I'm having fun. Now, I'm going to put my hand on your abdomen and I want you to push it out when you inhale."

"I don't think my lungs go down that far."

"That's because you Humans rarely use your full lung capacity. Breathe in through your nose and exhale through your nose and your mouth. Try not to raise your shoulders when you inhale. The idea is to evacuate more space in your body so the air will get pulled all the way down there."

"Am I moving your hand?"

"Yes, but try to do it with your breathing, not by pushing out your abdominal muscles."

Julie spent almost two minutes breathing in and out next to the Drazen before she realized that the alien rarely seemed to take a breath unless she was demonstrating. "How come you're not breathing with me?"

"Our metabolisms are more efficient than yours so we don't need to breathe as often unless we're expelling air by talking or singing. We actually have the best lung function of any of the oxygen-breathing species on the tunnel network. Our scientists claim it's a direct result of our singing tradition."

"How do you like teaching on Flower?" Julie asked, hoping to keep the Drazen girl talking in her musical voice.

"It's a bit lonely, actually. The only other Drazen women on board are all married with children, and the Humans who I teach have lives of their own. When I lived on Union Station and went to the Open University, I never understood how students from your species could walk around talking to the Stryx librarian about anything and everything. But since I've been here, I probably talk with Flower more than anybody else."

"You should come out with me sometime, I mean, if Drazens do things like that. I don't really know any girls my age either."

"I'd love to, and thank you for saying that, but I was probably your age before my parents let me out of the apartment on my own. We mature much slower than you do."

"Really? How long do you live?"

"I'm embarrassed to tell you," Rinka said and changed the subject. "Have you ever heard of solfège syllables?"

"Are they a Drazen thing?"

"They're Human, though I'm not sure which of your many warring cultures they came from. I took a survey course on Earth music at the Open University and it covered all of your systems for musical notation and voice teaching. I remember that one of your languages even has a verb to describe singing a passage in solfège that's derived from two of the syllables, Sol-Fa."

"I'm afraid I didn't understand all of that."

"How about this?" Rinka asked, and sang, "Do, Re, Mi, Fa, Sol, La, Ti, Do."

"That I get," Julie said with a smile.

"Flower and I made up a little song for the children to practice the solfège syllables. It goes like this:

Do – A Dollnick, a four-armed Dollnick
Re – A gun that shoots with light

Mi – Who me? You didn't see
Fa – A Farling taking flight
Sol – The star that you call home
La – It turns the sound down low
Ti – So the ball doesn't roam
That will bring us back to Do (Flower says so).

"Wait a second," Julie protested. "I'm sure I've heard it before with different lines."

"Ours are better," Flower informed her. "*La - A note to follow So?* Really?"

"How does 'La' turn the sound down low?"

"I've noticed that when your children don't want to hear something, they put their hands over their ears and sing, 'La, la, la, la, la.' I imagine they get it from their parents."

"Do you think you can sing it from memory?" Rinka asked Julie.

"Can I practice at home first?"

"You really are shy, aren't you? Alright, let's stick with warm-ups for today. You can just hum."

The Drazen sat back down at the piano and played a series of five notes that rose to a peak and then fell back for nine notes in total, all while humming along. "Now you."

"Uhm, uhm, uhm, uhm, uhm, uhm, uhm, uhm, uhm," Julie managed without blushing.

"Good. Now up one with Ahh," Rinka said, and started the sequence one note higher.

"Ahh, ahh, ahh, ahh, ahh, ahh, ahh, ahh, ahh."

"Excellent. Keep your jaw relaxed and try with Eee."

"Eee, eee, eee, eee, eee, eee, eee, eee, eee."

"Now put your hand on your diaphragm so you can feel the movement and we'll try staccato."

"What's that?"

"Making sharp separations between the notes. Like this."

The lesson continued with different exercises and vocalizations, and when Rinka informed her that their time was up, Julie couldn't believe a half-hour had gone by so quickly.

"I don't remember the last time I felt this good. What do I owe you and when's my next lesson?"

"This was the free try-out to see if you liked it," the Drazen girl said. "I normally keep an open slot after the travel chorus in case we go over time. Flower handles my bookings, so you can check your own schedule and work out open times with her."

"Great. What's a travel chorus?"

"The children you saw were the top singers from their classes. I have them for an hour every day after school to practice. If we were on a planet, the travel chorus would go to competitions, but instead we're going to put on performances at stops. It's still in the planning phase."

Eleven

"Is that some sort of game?" Irene asked her husband. She pointed at the giant display behind the steam table that normally showed an exterior view of Flower. Both of their heads began turning from side to side as they watched a glowing white ball pong back and forth between the two vertical paddles at opposing edges of the display. "It's sort of peaceful."

"I think it's supposed to be tennis, or maybe ping-pong," Harry said. "But where are the players?"

"It's a recording," Flower replied via the serving bot's speaker. "I thought it would help your new members from Bits feel at home."

"That's so thoughtful of you," Irene said. "I noticed that they've been keeping to themselves. Harry, we should eat with one of their groups tonight."

"I don't think there are any open spots at their tables," her husband replied, glancing at the seating area. "We signed up sixteen new members from Bits in the end, and they took over two tables of eight."

"Which makes it too late for you to join them for a bite," Flower cackled, and let out a whistle of untranslatable amusement at her own joke.

"I don't get it," Harry complained, aware only that the Dollnick AI was laughing at something. "What's so funny?"

"The new members are all old-fashioned computer enthusiasts from Bits, and there are eight bits in a byte. Get it?"

"Oh, that's really funny," Irene said politely. "What do you recommend today, Flower?"

"Try the vegetarian lasagna. I'm thinking of doing ethnic food nights once a week just to spice things up."

"That's a great idea. Back home, Harry and I belonged to a lodge that put on an international supper every month. I always liked the Italian food best, but he preferred Chinese. We had German, French, Japanese, Balkan, Polish, Greek—"

"It's all Greek to me," Flower interrupted, and the serving bot performed a drum roll in the air with its upper set of arms. "What, is my timing off? I thought that was a classic Human joke."

"Depends on the context," Harry said. "Are you planning on doing a stand-up routine? You'll have to come up with jokes that demand less of the audience."

"Or I could find a smarter audience."

"Suit yourself. How about Chinese for the first special dinner?"

"You need to think outside the box. When I said ethnic food, I meant from the different Human groups that have gone native. I've been reading through the new edition of the All Species Cookbook and I have to admit there may be something to the concept of providing the recipes in a living language. Your cooks on open worlds have done a clever job of coming up with look-alike dishes that pay homage to their hosts. I'm planning to start with Dollnick cuisine."

"Why doesn't that surprise me?"

"Just some peas to go with the main entrée," Irene said, and the bot deposited a measured ladleful on her plate. "I'm pretty certain that lasagna is from Earth, Flower."

"Do you think you were the first species in the universe to come up with broad, flat noodles layered with different proteins and vegetables? This is a popular recipe for Humans in Vergallian space because everything except for the cheese is from the local agricultural system."

"The Vergallian agricultural system? We can eat their food?"

"Some of it. Humans travelling in alien space are advised to order off the Vergallian vegan menu in a pinch."

"Bring me a tea," Irene requested of her husband. "I'm going to go find us a place."

Harry joined Dave at the hot drinks station and fixed his wife a cup of tea before pouring himself a coffee.

"Doesn't that keep you up at night?" Dave asked as he sorted through the herbal teabags.

"Caffeine never kept me from falling asleep, I guess it's a baker thing," Harry replied. "My doctor told me to stop drinking coffee with supper a few years back when I told him I was waking up at night, but it turned out not to make a difference."

"You mean to use the bathroom?"

"Once a man reaches a certain age, you have to assume it comes with the territory. As long as I don't wake up more than twice, I'm happy."

"I used to consider twice a good night," Dave said, finally locating the bag he was searching for. "No more."

"It's gotten worse?" Harry asked sympathetically.

"Better. I sleep like a baby."

"How'd you manage that?"

"How do you think?"

"Surgery?"

"I'm not sure, really," the older man confessed. "I used getting up at night as an excuse to go see the Farling doctor because I wanted to change his mind about the ice cream restriction he put on my nutrition chart. His end of the conversation went something like, 'I'll fix you for ten creds. Now drop your pants and tell me your favorite ice cream flavors.' I hadn't even gotten to pistachio before he was yelling 'Next' and pushing me out the door, but I haven't woken up at night since."

Harry followed the older man back to their usual table where Irene was sitting next to Brenda and took the seat next to his wife. "Where are Jack and Nancy?" he asked, noting the empty spots.

"On another dinner date, plus Jack said something about following up on a lead with his friend who runs a restaurant," Brenda informed them. "I see you took the lasagna too."

"Flower was pushing it. She probably made too much."

"It's good, though," Tom said to Harry. "You were right about the food in this place, but the ladies are a bit stand-offish."

"It's not us, it's you," Brenda told him. "If you could manage a complete sentence without leering, I'd consider letting you buy me a coffee just to hear about life on the Sharf recycling complex where you worked forty years."

"You know, that would make an interesting topic for a course in the continuing education program," Irene ventured. "Women for men who don't understand women."

Tom couldn't help responding with a leer, "I know what women want."

"I doubt that very much," Maureen said, taking the chair on Dave's other side. Somehow, with six out of eight seats taken, Tom found himself with an empty space on each side. "Tell me what I'm thinking right now."

By the time Harry and Irene finished their meal, Maureen had actually moved a seat closer to Tom so she wouldn't have to talk across an empty place.

"I'm beginning to think I shouldn't have recruited him," Harry said to his wife after they left the common room. "He's done nothing but chase after women since he came on board."

"He seems to be a good listener," Irene observed.

"That's because he's not stupid, and he knows if he opens his mouth, any intelligent woman would run the opposite direction." They entered the lift tube, and he said, "Amusement park."

"You're sure you want to come to work with me? I didn't mean to talk you into it. I just thought you might find it interesting."

"I want to understand how volunteering got you out of theatre practice tonight," Harry said. "It seems to me like Flower is making up the rules as she goes along."

"Flexibility is a sign of high intelligence," the Dollnick AI responded over the capsule speaker. "As it happens, this is an extra shift for your wife, so there has to be some kind of trade-off. Your theatre group is doing something different tonight as well."

"What's that?"

"You'll find out when you get there."

"My information booth assignment today is right next to the kiddie rides," Irene said, leading Harry out of the lift tube and past the long line queued up for the rollercoaster. "The carnies have been keeping a portion of the amusement park open since all those new people came aboard at Bits. They can't seem to get enough of the rides."

"Most of them have probably never been on one in their lives. Do you have your new tab in your purse?"

"I don't need it for this. There's an official ship's tab at the booth, and it's linked into the large display so that my clients can see what I see."

"Clients?"

"Information booth staff pride ourselves on our professionalism, even though we're all volunteers doing our community service. The training manual was over two-hundred pages long and there was an interactive test."

"Are you pulling my leg?" Harry demanded. "You crammed a two-hundred-page manual and passed a test in just a few days?"

"It was mainly pictures of aliens," Irene admitted. "Especially children. Some of the species go through a sort of metamorphosis as they mature so you can't go by the adults."

"But there aren't that many aliens on board and I doubt they're the sort to get lost in an amusement park or a bazaar."

"We do get alien guests when we stop at open worlds and other facilities where humans aren't the only occupants. We also get a lot of questions from people who have never seen a particular alien before and want to find out what species it is without acting rude."

"I suppose if that was the whole manual you'd do well because you've always had a good memory for faces."

"Yes, the alien pictures were much easier to recognize than the rides, which all look the same to me. Would you recognize a Zamperla Disco?"

"Not unless you dropped it on me while shouting the name."

"How about a Rampage Stampede or a Tivoli Tumbler?"

"I'd probably get motion sick looking at the pictures."

"That's right. You used to hide in the bakery when I took the kids to the state fair. What was that ride you liked at the local carnival?"

"The one with the giant teacups, but even Anna decided it was too boring for her when she turned eight."

"I'm surprised you remember the exact year."

"Don't forget that I made all of our kids those birthday cakes shaped like numbers when they were little so I have visual memory cues. Eight years old, chocolate layer cake, teacup ride."

"Are you my relief?" asked the woman working at the information booth as Irene approached.

"Yes. I brought my husband along to show him what we do. I'm Irene."

"Margret. I put everything that happened the last four hours in the log, but the main problem is that the same boy keeps running off and losing his family. The last time he was brought in by the fried dough vendor with the stand right at the edge of the food court."

"What's his name?"

"Hal, which must be very popular on Bits, because every time I make the announcement, a dozen parents who have lost sight of their own son for a minute show up." Margret finished untying her volunteer smock and passed it to Irene. "There aren't nearly as many people as the last few days. I asked a couple of the parents about it, and apparently there's some kind of big competition going on that a lot of the Bitters are participating in."

139

Irene tied on the smock that identified her as an information booth specialist and took her place between the giant display and the small postern that held an official ship's tab.

"No chair?" Harry asked. "Don't you get tired of standing?"

"I would if I stood in one place, but I move around the booth. There's a chair that folds out of the bulkhead if I want to sit down. Ask me something so I can demonstrate how the system works."

"Uh, where's the roller coaster?"

"Seriously? We just walked past the line on the way here and you could see it if you turned around. Ask me something hard."

"Didn't we just discuss my ignorance of all things related to amusement parks?"

"Then ask me something about the bazaar."

"That's an idea. I've been meaning to look for an insulated coffee cup with a lid like I used to have back in college."

"Whatever for?"

"So I can make coffee at home and bring it to work with me."

"Doesn't Flower have a coffee maker in the kitchen?"

"It's not the same as my old one," Harry said stubbornly.

Irene sighed and addressed herself to the tab. "My client is looking for a travel mug for hot beverages."

The giant display behind her lit up with a map view of a section of the bazaar where a number of booths were highlighted as possible matches for the query. The control tab showed the same image, and Irene tapped on a likely-looking candidate labeled "Ellen's Galaxy of Mugs." The view changed to high-resolution video.

"Whoa," Harry said, flinching at the motion blur.

"Are those what you're talking about?" his wife asked, pausing with the view on a collection of lidded travel mugs.

"Bingo. I'll take the silver one. How much are they?"

"It's not a catalog, Harry. You have to go there and buy it yourself."

"Where is it?"

Irene tapped something on the tab which reverted the image to map mode, and then she pulled back the field of view. "It's way on the other side of the bazaar, maybe a twenty-minute walk from here if you don't get lost. But I don't see any people moving around so they probably aren't open." She tapped a different control and a colored overlay appeared that blocked out almost every one of the vendor stands. "I was afraid of that. Most of the specialty sellers are only open for a few hours around lunch between stops unless you make a special appointment. I'll buy a mug for you next time I work the floor during a stop."

A heavily tattooed older man with a small boy in tow approached the couple. "Dropping off," the carny said.

"Is he lost?"

"I caught him trying to crawl under the carousel. Kids don't realize how dangerous it is under there."

"Let me go," the boy demanded, twisting and turning, but the man looked strong enough to hold a horse.

"What's your name?" Irene asked the boy.

"Hal," he said in a surly voice. "And I'm not lost."

"Do you know where your parents are?"

Hal shrugged. "They were on the stupid teacups ride the last I saw. That's for children."

"And how old are you?" Irene asked.

"Six," the boy said, drawing himself up to his full height. "Let me go. I have rights."

"Do you promise not to crawl under the rides?"

"Promise," the boy said with a scowl.

Irene nodded to the tattooed man who released his catch, and the boy scurried off in the direction of the rollercoaster.

"Morton," the man said, offering his hand to Harry. "They won't let him on the rollercoaster. He's not tall enough."

"Harry, and this is my wife, Irene. You work with the rides?"

"I own some of them and I keep the rest running. It's sort of a specialty these days."

"I imagine fixing carnival rides in space doesn't come up that often, other than on Flower," Irene said.

"I've been with the circuit ship since the beginning so I've had the chance to visit alien amusement parks on some of the open worlds where we stop," Morton said. "Their rides are so well engineered that they hardly require any maintenance. The rides in here are all from Earth, and even now that they're out of the weather, the wear parts need constant attention."

"So you joined the ship directly from Earth?" Harry asked.

"First cruise. They wanted to buy my rides and I made myself part of the bargain. Between the falling population and all of those self-driving floaters that can zip a family to a major theme park while they sleep, traveling fairs and carnivals were dying out. Another year or two and most of my rides would have been piles of rust."

"I always got motion sick on anything that went up and down or back and forth. If you'd told me a couple of months ago that I'd be retiring to a giant centrifuge, I'd never have believed it."

"It's all a question of scale," Morton explained. "If you try to spin a little ship in space to make weight, your head ends up weighing less than your feet, and that's enough to make anybody nauseous. Flower is big enough that it feels like living on a planet."

"Have you ever had this much business between stops before?" Irene asked. "When Flower requested I come in for an extra shift, she said that the enthusiasm of the Bitters for the amusement park took her by surprise."

"Normally we only operate a few of the children's rides between stops, and those on a limited schedule because the demand just isn't there. I imagine that once the crowd from Bits gets all settled in things will go back to normal. Flower is a cagey old AI, though. Based on the questions she's been asking me about my maintenance schedules, I suspect that she'd eventually like to keep this deck humming around the clock, whether we're stopped or not."

"But where would the customers come from?"

"She'd need to scare up a lot of passengers or permanent residents to make it work, but I imagine if we had a few million people on board, this place would be minting money. I told Flower about season passes and she asked me to bring it up with the other carnies at our next meeting."

"How can you have season passes without seasons?" Irene asked.

"We'll call a circuit a season, or maybe split it into the Earth-to-Union Station and back segments—that would be around three months. But it would give people a reason to come every day, and if they've invested in a season pass, that's one more reason to stay on board. If the ride owners see a drop in revenue, Flower is offering to make up the difference in rent remission."

"I guess she really is leaving no stone left unturned in trying to boost the population."

"It was nice meeting you, Morton," Harry said, "but I have to get to theatre practice. Irene, don't work too hard, and sit if you get tired."

"I used to stand behind the counter at the bakery for ten hours a day if you've forgotten," Irene reminded him. "A four-hour shift is like being on vacation."

Twelve

"We must be at the wrong theatre," Bill said, stepping back from the door, which whooshed closed again. "Ask Flower over your implant."

"You have one now too," Julie reminded him.

"I keep forgetting," he said, and asked out loud, "Flower?"

"Why are you standing outside? In two minutes, you'll almost be late."

"Somebody else is using our theatre. There're thousands of people in there."

"The director is waiting for you on the stage."

"I'm not getting up in front of all of those people and rehearsing a play about Grenouthian documentaries!"

"The director dropped that idea after visiting Timble and I wouldn't advise bringing it up again in his hearing. Now don't be such a scaredy-cat and go see what it's all about. Jorb and some of the others you know from the cafeteria are waiting."

"The alien spies are joining our theatre group?"

Harry approached the pair and said, "Good evening, Julie, Bill. Why are you waiting out here?"

"The theatre is standing room only."

"But it's built to hold five thousand Dollnicks!"

"That's what I'm saying."

"Come on, guys," Julie said with a sigh. "You know that Flower is going to talk us into going in there eventually so we may as well be on time and get credit. I think I know what this is all about."

Bill steeled himself and stepped forward again. The doors slid open on a crowd of hooting and hollering people, many of whom were easily identified by their fanciful outfits as having joined the ship at Bits. The long walk down the aisle seemed to take forever, but it gave the three of them time to realize that all of the attention was on the holograms floating at the front of the theatre, and the aliens on the stage weren't even visible.

"This must be the character competition for Flower's new animation production company that Zick was telling me about," Julie informed the other two, half-shouting to make herself heard.

"Who's Zick?" Bill shouted back.

"A guy from Bits who came into the library and then stopped by the diner today. You'll like him."

"You'll hate him," Flower said over Bill's implant. "He's interested in Julie."

As soon as they reached the stage, the noise from the large audience was greatly reduced, a sure sign that an audio suppression field was in use.

"Are the three of you it?" the Grenouthian demanded of the new arrivals.

"My wife is volunteering at the amusement park tonight," Harry said defensively. "Flower approved it."

"I was asking about the rest of your theatre team."

"We don't know where they are," Julie said. "Maybe the crowd scared them off."

"No matter, I've only seen three Human chars I can work with in any case. And since you and Bill now have implants and Harry is wearing his ear cuff, I can get rid of this annoying external translator," the director added, snapping the ribbon that held it around his neck and dropping the pendant in his pouch. "You missed all of the preliminary rounds to winnow down the choices, and we're working through the elimination rounds for each species now. Humans are already finished."

"So what are we doing here?" Harry asked.

"Storyboarding. Grenouthian style. From tonight on you're all working as stand-ins."

"I thought the job of a stand-in was to hold an actor's place for technical purposes."

"That's substantially correct. You'll be standing in for Gerryman."

"As in gerrymandering?"

"As in geriatric. Flower and I have been studying the entertainment demographics for your species and I'm convinced that an older superhero will go over big. Julie, you're a natural for Refill."

"Who?"

"She's a superhero who uses waitressing skills to un-cover evildoers and defeat their schemes," the bunny said. "Bill, you'll be Digger."

"What kind of superhero digs?"

The director shrugged his furry shoulders. "The Bitters presented so many characters that dig, we felt compelled to select at least one of them. Apparently there are a large number of legacy Earth games featuring miners."

"But how does a miner defeat his enemies?" Bill com-plained.

"Hit 'em with a shovel," Jorb advised. "Or you could dig holes for them to fall into."

"What did you get, Razood?"

"The Blacksmith," the Frunge said, puffing out his chest. "When I saw the char, it was like a match made in heaven. Who knew your people had such talent as illustrators?"

"And you want us to stand in for holograms?" Harry asked incredulously.

"Not holograms, three-dimensional anime," the bunny corrected him. "Well, technically they are holograms, but anime has its own ecosystem, with dedicated award shows and distribution channels."

"I wasn't complaining about the technology, I just don't see why you would need live actors to stand in for computer-generated cartoon figures."

"Anime," the Grenouthian director growled, and Harry raised his hands shoulder-high in a sign of submission. "And the reason for using live stand-ins is to save money. Do you have any idea how expensive a single minute of 3D rendering can cost?"

"But Flower could probably do it in her sleep. She faked a whole ballroom scene to advertise our independent living cooperative."

"She reprocessed existing content and pasted-in your faces. Creating live-action holograms on the fly is child's play for the Stryx, but it would present a serious drain on Flower's spare capacity."

"I'm Slomo," the Verlock spoke up ponderously. "My char moves in slow motion and his superpower is that he can force everybody else to slow down to match him."

"Did you just make that last part up?" the director asked. "I like it. It will cut down on the production costs because we can reduce the overall frame rate whenever you're in the hologram."

"I'm Battle Royale," the stunning Vergallian who operated the finishing school informed the late arrivals. "A rogue queen with an unquenchable thirst for men."

"Combat," the Grenouthian corrected her. "An unquenchable thirst for combat."

"Whatever."

"Who are you?" Bill asked Jorb.

"I don't have a char yet. They're just getting to the Drazens now."

Above their heads, over a hundred holograms of Drazen characters appeared in fanciful garb, all bearing special weapons or tools.

"Make it Axe Man, make it Axe Man," Jorb muttered rapidly under his breath. "Not Juggler, not Juggler."

"I thought you just said that projecting holograms was too demanding for Flower," Harry said to the bunny.

"Projection is simple, the theatre equipment handles that. It's creating the data for high-resolution animated holograms that requires intensive processing," the director explained. "These chars have already been rendered and the creators are streaming them to the projection system. Can't you see that the anime aren't interacting with each other?"

The Drazen with the axe who Jorb was rooting for took a roundhouse swing with the weapon that cut through several neighboring anime without having any effect.

"So how do you pick a winner?" Julie asked.

"It's not about winning and losing," Flower replied over the girl's implant. "It's about storytelling. Which of the chars says something to you?"

"It's a tough angle to judge from," Julie hedged. "The Drazen acrobat juggling knives while doing tentacle stands looks kind of interesting."

"That's the one I picked," Flower said.

"Juggler," the Grenouthian director agreed. He made the announcement and all of the other holograms disappeared, leaving the acrobatic character alone to work through his extensive routine of pre-programmed moves.

Jorb groaned and wrapped his tentacle over his eyes so he wouldn't have to watch.

"Now comes my favorite part," Flower told Julie.

"Dollnicks?" the girl guessed immediately.

A new set of characters appeared, all sporting four arms and feathered crests. It quickly became apparent that the computational models underlying movement generation for the alien anime were based on two-armed humanoids, because the lower set of arms on most of the figures moved awkwardly, if at all.

"I don't like any of them," Lume said, crossing all four of his arms across his body. "I never thought I'd envy Brynlan his Slomo character, but it's better than standing in for an obvious marionette."

"They are rather disappointing," the Grenouthian agreed. "Maybe we could commission a new character designed by the joint winners for the other species."

"Thinker isn't bad," Harry observed, pointing to the seated character whose artist had reinterpreted Rodin's iconic sculpture so that the hands of the Dollnick's upper arms were under his chin, while the hands of both his lower arms gripped his kneecaps. "I was never a big comic book fan, but he could be the brains behind the outfit."

"A stay-behind mastermind," Lume mused. "I could live with that. It would certainly make for easy stand-in work."

"Is Flower paying all of you for this?"

"She waived my volunteering requirement, or maybe it was my team sport. It's getting hard to keep track since she's always asking for favors."

"So if all the characters are picked out, are we done for today?" Julie asked.

"Were you planning on standing in from home?" the director inquired genially. "After we pick the character I'll be standing in for and an initial supervillain, I'll want you all for the next hour so I can start working on the promo."

"You can direct and stand in?"

"I'm multi-talented."

The holographic display switched to Grenouthians, and it suddenly became much lighter in the theatre because every last designer had chosen white fur. Several of the animations hopped around like kangaroos, but most remained in place working through karate-type exercises.

"That's a tough-looking bunch of bunnies," Bill couldn't help observing. "What's with the one playing the weird instrument?"

"That's not a musical instrument, it's a type of traditional abacus used by our traders," the director informed him. "I think he's the best of the bunch."

"A superhero accountant? What's he going to do? Bring the production in under budget?"

"The Producer," Brynlan pronounced. "A valuable asset."

Flower must have agreed, because all of the holograms except for the abacus-wielding bunny disappeared, and then one by one, the other winners began popping into view. There was a Frunge blacksmith with a massive hammer, a human wearing a hardhat with a shovel over his shoulder, Slomo the Verlock, a dangerous-looking waitress with a steaming pot of coffee, Juggler, who was keeping a glittering arc of knives airborne, Gerryman, who hobbled forward leaning on a cane and then deployed it as a spinning shield, Brains, the four-armed thinker, and finally Battle Royale, with her gravity-defying bosom barely held in check by a scanty halter top.

Flower gave the winning chars a few minutes to exhaust their pre-programmed library of moves for the cheering crowd before announcing, "And now we'll move on to our starting supervillain."

"Let me be a Drazen villain," Jorb begged. "I don't want to play an acrobat."

"Maybe Juggler is a superhero during the day and a villain at night," Razood suggested. "It's been known to happen."

"Are you guys all cartoon fans?" Julie asked as a new collection of holograms began popping into existence overhead. "I thought they were for kids."

"Anime," the Grenouthian director repeated in a tired voice. "The visual storytelling has many similarities to theatre."

"Why did all their faces start glowing?" Bill asked, pointing out at the crowd.

"The Bitters are powering on their tabs to vote for the villains," Razood told his apprentice. "We did the same thing in the preliminary rounds for superheroes."

"I thought Flower and the director were picking the characters."

"They are, but it doesn't hurt to get an opinion from the audience, and it keeps them involved."

"The voting is rigged?" Bill asked.

"No comment," Flower said over his implant. "What do you think of the giant insect with all of the pincers?"

"He reminds me a little of the doctor."

"That's perfect. Most people have an unconscious fear of Farlings. The only problem will be getting him to stand in."

"He's too busy?"

"Too expensive," Flower groused. "Director?"

"The bug is the best of the bunch," the Grenouthian concurred. "What did the voting show?"

"The teenage girl in the school uniform with the katana. You can see why I don't take Human votes seriously."

"You're only picking one villain?" Harry asked. "It doesn't seem fair, not to mention limiting the dramatic possibilities."

"I want to have the first episode ready in three months, and the last thing we need is too many plot complications," the Dollnick AI responded. "Besides, supervillains have minions."

"Speaking of time, we have less than an hour left," the director said. "Do you have a strategy for getting all of those Humans to leave?"

"Just watch me," Flower said, and gave a shrill whistle through the theatre's public address system. "All of today's competitors have demonstrated excellent skills and I intend to provide work for each and every one of you. As a special thanks for participating in our contest, I've issued instructions to the owners of all the bars and restaurants on board. For the next two hours, anybody presenting a ticket to today's event is entitled to free drinks and desserts. Furthermore—"

The rest of the announcement was drowned out by the roar of the crowd and the thudding of spring-loaded seats folding themselves back into the closed position as everybody surged for the exits. It was a testament to the many years the Bitters had spent conducting evacuation drills from compromised domes that nobody got trampled in the mad rush.

"So, what did you and Flower have in mind for a storyline?" Lume asked the director. "How about something that starts with a rift in the space-time continuum that connects our galaxy with an evil mirror galaxy?"

"That's been done a hundred times," the bunny responded. "All we've decided so far is that we want a story compatible with showing off our production capabilities."

"It's my first time in the entertainment business and I don't want to invest heavily on modeling interior scenes, so we'll set the story on an unidentified Dollnick colony ship," Flower announced. "In that sense, I'll be standing in with the rest of you."

"If you don't even have the vague outline worked out, how can we stand in for characters this evening?" Harry asked.

"The first step in the production process is to release some stills showing off the chars and costumes so that the anime community will have something to speculate about."

"Is this different than the guerilla marketing plan you told me about?" Bill asked, half raising his hand.

"It all fits together. Let's get the promo shots out of the way. Director?"

"Everybody who knows how to guide a floating immersive camera, bring one out from backstage," the Grenouthian director instructed. "We'll position them around ourselves for full 3D capture to give the animators something they can flesh out."

Harry followed the other aliens backstage to retrieve a camera, leaving Bill and Julie alone on the stage in the rapidly emptying theatre.

"You knew what this was about when we came in?" Bill asked.

"I met the guy who designed the Slomo char," Julie replied. "Zick said that he's a writer too, so maybe he'll help with the story."

"Do you think people will be able to recognize us after the animators turn us into cartoons?"

"Anime, and I hope not. Flower?"

"If the likeness makes you uncomfortable, you can always deny it," the Dollnick AI said. "Besides, this could turn into your big break."

"You mean we could have a career working as animation stand-ins?" Bill asked.

"It doesn't pay that well. But as the director said, the anime community is very active, with fans from all of the species and amazing cosplay conventions. You know what? I think I'll host one."

"What's cosplay?"

"Costume play. It's performance art for fans."

"Why would I want to go to a cosplay convention? I hate dressing up."

"If my production does as well as I intend, being known as the stand-in for one of the chars could prove very lucrative, especially if the resemblance is apparent. Fans will pay to have their pictures taken with you."

"I don't know about this," Julie said. "I've been famous once already for the wrong reason."

"Move to the center of the stage," the director instructed on his return. He had two floating immersive cameras under his control, yet was still able to gesture without crashing them. "The rest of you set the cameras on independent hover and I'll handle the final placements."

Harry and the group of alien spies joined Bill and Julie standing awkwardly at the center of the stage. The giant bunny moved rapidly around them, positioning the cameras and occasionally peering at the grouping over a furry thumb.

"Props are here," Flower announced, and a pair of maintenance bots floated on stage with a large theatrical chest suspended between them. "Razood, you're the weapons master so you hand out the prizes."

The Frunge blacksmith flipped up the lid and immediately began tossing items over his shoulder without looking, though they all ended up on target. "Bill. Hard hat. Brynlan. Ninja costume, extra-large. Jorb. Hatchet. Hatchet. Hatchet. Hatchet," he called, tossing the axes behind him. The Drazen martial artist reluctantly caught each one and kept them airborne in a glittering arc.

"I thought you couldn't juggle," Julie said.

"I don't want to be known for playing a character called Juggler. There's a difference."

"Mine," Razood declared, drawing out a hammer that must have weighed more than a small child. "Gerryman," he continued, and turning his head, gently tossed Harry a wooden cane. "Going by the weight, I think it's got a sword in it."

"Where's my weapons harness?" Avisia demanded.

"Kit for Battle Royale," Razood said, pulling out the leather halter top with loops carrying all sorts of deadly-looking throwing weapons. He handed it to her and motioned for Julie to accompany him back to the chest. "I didn't want to throw this either," he said, offering her a glass coffeepot with an orange handle. "And here's the tray."

"Decaf?" she demanded incredulously. "Am I supposed to put my enemies to sleep?"

"And here's your shovel at the bottom," he said, drawing the tool out for Bill. "The folding chair must be for you, Lume."

"Where's my abacus?" the director demanded.

"Check the pocket under the lid," Flower said. "I had to send a bot to borrow it from the Grenouthians with the bazaar booth, and they insisted I treat it like an antique."

"Can you do something about the lighting, Flower?" the director requested. "Too many shadows." He hopped around the group, in one case lowering his bulk to the floor to inspect everything from toe-top level, and finally entered the ring of cameras to join the others. "Small stand-ins to the front, large to the rear. Harry and Julie, you stand to either side of Lume."

"He's huge," Harry pointed out.

"I'll be sitting," the Dollnick said, deploying his folding chair and assuming the four-armed thinker position.

"Harry, pull a little of that blade out of the cane, and Julie, bend your wrist like you're throwing a pot of hot coffee in somebody's face. Great overhead swing stance, Razood, and Jorb, grab one of those hatchets with your tentacle, will you? Choke up on the shovel, Bill, and everybody look fierce. Cameras on," he issued the voice command.

"Perfect," Flower said a minute later. "I can see it all coming together."

"That's a take," the director concluded. "Those of you taking the theatre sport, if you see any of your other team members, tell them it's on hold until Flower finds them a new director. This project is going to require all of my time."

157

Thirteen

A young man with a yellow umbrella was waiting for the members of the independent living cooperative when they exited the shuttle. "Are you the group from Flower's Paradise?" he inquired.

"Sixty-eight of us," Jack replied. "Don't let these two young ones throw you off."

"I'm Dianne, from the Galactic Free Press," the reporter identified herself. "I hitched a ride and I'll be accompanying the group on their tour to write a story. I'm remaining on the ground after they return so I can work on some other articles."

"You're posted here?" the guide asked.

"Just until the ship is ready to leave."

"Grab me at the end of the day and I'll introduce you to the head archeologist from the human contingent," the young man said. "And who are you?" he asked, turning to Julie.

"Refill," the girl responded, striking her superhero pose with an imaginary tray and coffee pot. "Just kidding. I'm Julie and I'm here to carry things and run errands for the cooperative."

"Great. So I'm Joab, and I'll be taking you to the volunteer site. Our standard one-day program starts with some hands-on work at the dig, followed by lunch, and then there's a three-hour walking tour. You've prepaid for the tour, but lunch is extra."

"Are we working in the morning because it gets too hot in the afternoon?" Nancy asked.

"Our day here is a little over forty hours so we pretty much ignore the local clock," Joab explained. "We used to start with the tour but we found that our visitors often looked disappointed when they boarded their shuttles to leave. Then we swapped the volunteer stint in the dig to the first half of the day and everybody seemed happier."

"Is the work that hard?" Harry asked. "We're no spring chickens, as you can see."

"It's mainly brushing ash away with a paintbrush," the guide said, walking backwards towards the excavation site that stretched into the distance. "You have to go through a three-day training course before they'll let you use a shovel, five days if you want to swing a pick."

"Are they afraid of liability if volunteer workers hurt themselves?" Brenda asked.

"That happens all the time anyway when people dig by hand. The training is to protect buried artifacts and structures," Joab said, then launched into a prepared speech. "The first step for an archeological dig is to survey the target area with ground-penetrating radar, sonar, and a few alien imaging techniques that I don't really understand. This gives the archeologists a pretty detailed map of what we're going to find, but you need training in reading the three-dimensional maps accurately before anybody is going to let you go at it with a trowel, much less a shovel."

"So you're saying there's about zero chance that we'll be making any discoveries?" Irene asked, keeping the floating camera she was operating focused on the young guide.

"Sometimes small items slip by the imaging screens. For example, coins and personal ornamentation can be difficult to differentiate from certain types of small rocks or naturally occurring nuggets. When I take you for lunch at the visitor center, you'll see a display of artifacts that tourists have uncovered. It's just not very likely."

"You mean if I find something valuable I won't get to keep it?" Tom demanded. "I worked in recycling most of my career, and it was industry standard practice to let the workers retain any coins or jewelry we found in the cushions of old acceleration couches."

"You'll have to complain to the Stryx, they're the ones who make the rules here," Joab said. "After the initial survey is complete, we set up a grid with string that can be referenced to a fixed point, so we can accurately establish the original location of any artifacts that we remove. It's safety string that will break before it trips you, but we'd prefer if you didn't test it. Once the grids are established, the trained excavators dig test pits with picks and shovels, and we sift through all of the removed material, a job that some of you will be assigned this morning. Then the archeologists select areas from the imaging that they want fully exposed, and when the trowel crew reaches any of the target objects, they call in the brush crew to remove the rest of the overlay."

"You're saying you dig out items by whisking away the dirt?" Harry asked. "That could take days."

"It's compacted ash, not dirt, and it usually takes an hour or so unless you're talking about something really large. You can use the dumb end of the paintbrush to dig a little, but if you get caught really jabbing it in, the grid supervisor will move you to work sifting."

"You've mentioned ash a couple of times," Nancy said. "Was this site buried by an ancient volcanic eruption like Pompeii?"

"Is that one of those Verlock worlds where they misjudged the volcanic activity?" Joab asked, still walking backwards.

"No, it's a city on Earth that was buried in the times of the Roman Empire."

The former school teacher's answer finally brought Joab to a temporary halt. "Are you talking about the aliens from one of those ancient SciFi series my dad watches?"

"The Romans were—"

"I remember now," Joab cut her off, resuming his backwards walk. "My mom made me memorize all the important stuff from Earth's history. The Romans came between the Greeks and the Mongols, right?"

"That's accurate as far as it goes, but they were hardly the only civilizations."

"I mainly liked the military empires. Anyway, if, uh, Pompeii had been anything like this place, humanity would have been extinct before the Stryx opened Earth."

"Is that what happened here?" Dianne asked.

"Around a million years ago," the guide continued. "This world got the double-whammy, and there's a big round ocean where most of the water ended up when it was all over. After the asteroid strike, the planet went into a long phase of hyper-volcanic activity, and everything that hadn't already been wiped out got buried in ash."

"But it looks so green," Irene said.

"The plants are the first to come back," Joab said. "Seeds and microbes are pretty tough, but none of the big land fauna made it, and the ocean isn't exactly teeming with life either." He came to a halt right before his heel reached the grid string at the edge of the excavation. "The poor aliens who lived here were barely into their iron age when it happened, but there were a lot of them, and they were great at building with stone. The Stryx declared the world a Galactic Heritage site, and they only opened it to excavation a decade ago. There are around two million people employed on the planet, which is how we got into CoSHC. More than half of us work on the dig, and there are also around a thousand aliens, but almost all of them are scientists or students."

"How long have you been here?"

"Since the beginning. My parents brought me here when I was eleven." Joab reached in his shoulder pouch and pulled out a handful of what looked like artist's brushes. "Now who wants to work squatting or kneeling, and who wants to sift through the excavated material?"

Nearly three hours had passed with nobody discovering anything more exciting than shards of pottery, when Maureen, who had been cleaning off the remains of a stone hearth with a paintbrush, cried out, "Over here. I think I found something."

Joab was the first one to arrive and he immediately spotted the glint of gold she had uncovered. He used his own paintbrush to clear a little more of the ash away and then utilized his tab to take a still image of the small coin before lifting it out with the blunt end of his brush.

"Congratulations," the young guide said. "You're the first tourist this month to find a coin."

"It's so thin," Maureen marveled.

"Is gold common on this world?" Tom asked.

"No more so than on Earth," Joab said. "If you're wondering how gold coins could end up lying around like that, I've got two explanations. First, most of the stone structures on this world were knocked flat in the asteroid impact and the quakes that followed. Second, enough microbes and bacteria survived and adapted to break down the organics that were buried in the ash, but the gold wasn't affected."

"Could you put the coin back for a minute and let Maureen find it again?" Irene asked. "It would make a great scene for our promo."

Joab smiled at the request, and he skillfully reburied the coin, brushing a little ash over the top. "Go for it," he told Maureen. "Just don't mention this to anybody at the gift shop. In addition to selling replica coins, they have a little studio with a fake excavation set up so you can record your find and fool your friends."

"Why would anybody want to do that?" Irene asked as the first glint of gold appeared on the camera's viewfinder screen.

"I've never been a tourist so I couldn't say. Are you all ready for lunch?"

Although the weather was temperate, and Julie had done her job bringing around water to make sure the cooperative members stayed hydrated, everybody had had enough of sifting or brushing ash by that point. Joab led them to the visitor center, opening his yellow umbrella along the way.

"Remember, yellow," he told them. "I'm going to eat with the other guides, but I'll be back in forty-five minutes."

Jack carefully climbed onto a stone bench at the entry to the visitor center and let out a shrill whistle to get everybody's attention. "We made a deal in advance with the cafeteria management for a group discount, and Julie is going to get our vouchers. You can get in line now, and she'll come around and give everybody their chit before you reach the checkout. We only have forty-five minutes before the walking tour starts, so please don't wander off after you eat."

There were still plenty of open tables when the cooperative members began looking for seats, and they ended up arranging themselves in their traditional lunch groupings.

"It's easy to forget how good we have it on Flower," Nancy said, moving aside a leaf of limp lettuce to reveal a mealy slice of tomato. "We should have taken her up on her offer to send a picnic lunch for two creds a head."

"Places like this don't like it if you bring your own food," Jack pointed out. "Besides, it's for a good cause."

"Do you think the profits go to the preservation work?"

"I read the health certificate while we were waiting in line, and the cafeteria is managed by a business that won an auction for a five-year contract. But the cafeteria's profitability establishes the auction price, and that money does go to the Stryx for running the dig."

"I'll eat that salad if you don't want it," Dave volunteered.

"Why didn't you get soup or a sandwich?" Nancy asked.

"I don't want to blow my diet. I'm trying to earn back my ice cream privilege."

"I think I saw a compost bin outside," Harry said. "I'm not one to waste food, but this quiche is only fit for recycling."

"Have my half-sandwich," Irene offered, pushing her plate to her husband. "The soup already ruined my appetite."

"We really are spoiled," Jack said. "The only thing wrong with this food is that it's average."

"I'd rather browse through the displays before the tour starts," Harry said. But he took his wife up on her offer to eat the diagonally sliced half of a cheese sandwich on wheat. "Edible," he muttered. "Barely."

"Isn't that the young man who works for you in the kitchen?" Irene asked, pointing towards the table occupied by the tour guides. Harry looked up and saw Bill handing a package to Joab, who used his butter knife to cut it open.

"He must be making a delivery for the new business Flower started. I can't wrap my head around the economics of what they're doing based on the way he explained it to me."

"What's so complicated about package delivery?"

"It sounded to me like rather than charging for postage or freight cost, they buy the packages from the sender in exchange for fruit, and then sell them to the recipient for cash," Harry explained.

"That's an interesting business model," Dave said. "If you're serious about making a sale, there's no better way than showing up in person with the goods. Back in the day, I sold more samples out of my kit than I took orders for custom units."

"What did you sell?"

"Pretty much everything at one time or another. I was a professional salesman, not somebody who got stuck doing it because the business didn't have anybody else. I was a millionaire before I was forty, though that was e-bucks, not creds."

"What did you spend it all on?"

"Whatever junk anybody tried to sell me," Dave replied with a laugh. "There's nobody easier to sell to than a salesman."

"I would have thought the opposite," Harry said. "You know all the tricks."

"There aren't any tricks, other than timing your closing proposition. What made me a great salesman was that I always believed in the products I represented, and when I found something I could believe in even more, I moved along. But I never sold real estate, and it was timeshares that ruined my personal finances. It seemed like such a great idea, owning a share of different places where I'd want to spend a few weeks a year. My goal was to own a slice of enough different condos that I could always live where the weather was nice."

"That sounds like a good plan," Jack said. "What went wrong?"

"Pretty much everything. As Earth's population kept dropping, the businesses managing these places had to keep on raising the maintenance fees on the members who didn't default. By the end, the value of the individual timeshares was zero, and the management was happy to get anybody who would cover the fees. On top of that, I underestimated the cost of flying from place to place every other week. Then my health started giving me problems, and with all the doctor visits, scheduling became a nightmare. I had fun for a decade or two, but I burned through all of my savings."

"And now you get to travel the galaxy without ever leaving home," Nancy said. "I read an old novel about wealthy people who lived permanently on luxury ocean liners, crossing back and forth between Europe and North America."

"Why would anybody do that?" Harry asked.

"Supposedly the food was very good."

"If everybody is finished, why don't we take a look through the displays as a group so we won't have to wait for strays when the tour starts," Jack suggested.

"How about the gift shop?" somebody asked.

"Don't worry. If there's one thing I'm sure of it's that nobody gets off this planet without going through the gift shop."

The time for their tour to start came and went without the guide appearing. Jack delegated Harry to check the restrooms while he went to ask at the table where Joab had last been seen. The baker was too old to bend low enough to look for feet in the stall with the locked door, and he was about to give up when he heard a loud beeping.

"Are you okay in there?" Harry called, knocking on the door.

"I just got killed again," a voice complained. "Go away."

"Is that you, Joab?"

"No."

"It is you. Open the door and let's get going. You owe us a tour."

The toilet flushed, and then the reluctant guide came out, still looking down at the portable game system he held in his hand. "I forgot how much I hated this thing," Joab said. "It's addictive. I broke it the first time by throwing it at a wall. It's your fault for bringing it back to me."

"Our fault?"

"Well, your ship, so it is your fault, sort of."

"Just put it away," Harry suggested. "You're going to fall into an excavation if you try walking backwards, talking, and playing games at the same time."

"I can do this," the guide insisted.

Three hours later, Harry had to admit that the kid had done a reasonable job of giving a tour without ever looking up to watch where he was going, and somehow Joab even managed to answer their questions. The endless beeps coming from the game even came in handy when they entered the underground portion of the site, a network of tunnels that had only recently been excavated.

"That's it," Joab informed them when the group arrived back at the gift shop. "Any other questions?"

"Are there retired workers living near the dig site?" Nancy inquired. "We like to spread the good word about living on board Flower when the opportunity arises."

"It's an active excavation site, so the only non-workers are children and family members. Since the world is sponsored by the Stryx, they offer free transportation to anywhere on the tunnel network for employees who complete their contracts."

"Flower is going to be disappointed," Dave said.

"Don't worry," Harry told him. "Flower mentioned that her favorite part about visiting interesting places with lots of humans is she can fill the shuttle seats in both directions."

Fourteen

The Frunge blacksmith called his part-time apprentice over to the display table. "They want a demonstration of the mace. I'll hold up the target and you try not to miss this time."

Bill choked up on the mace while Razood used a grease pencil to draw a small circle in an unmarked area of the badly pitted surface of a metal-clad practice shield. Summoning up all of the instructions that his employer had drummed into his head, Bill kept both eyes open and focused on the target as he followed through with an overhand swing. The wiry blacksmith allowed the muscles of his arms to absorb the shock, and then flipped the shield to inspect the damage.

"Close," he said, examining the new dent and perforation that fell right on the grease line. Then the Frunge blacksmith handed the shield over to his potential customers, game designers who joined the ship at Bits.

"So, even though the raised ridges on the mace head aren't that sharp, they punched through the metal," the taller customer said, running his finger across the dent.

"The steel cladding was stretched to the failing point in a small area," Razood confirmed. "Personally, I can't imagine why anybody would choose to fight in full plate armor for exactly that reason, but I understand it was popular with wealthy knights at one point in your history."

"Better a dent in your armor than a hole in your body," the other game designer observed.

"Not necessarily," the blacksmith told him. "Imagine you're in the middle of a battle and you now have a dimple of metal plate crushed into your body and you can't even take the armor off. And no matter how well balanced a suit of plate armor, it's going to put limits on your mobility. I saw a Grenouthian documentary about a famous battle that took place on your world less than a millennium ago. Thousands of armored men were basically immobilized in waist-deep mud, and many drowned or were slaughtered with ranged weapons. In the end, the best defense is a good offense."

"We'll take the mace," said the taller man who had requested the demonstration. "As to the price, can you sharpen your pencil a little?"

Razood looked down at the grease stick he had used to draw the target. "It works fine as is."

"I meant, could you come down on the two-hundred-cred price? My team has a three-hundred-cred budget for new maces to model for the next game update and we were hoping to buy a spiked ball mace as well."

"Some people call them flails," the other game designer put in.

Razood looked to Bill. "Do you know what they're talking about?"

"I'm not a weapons guy," the apprentice protested.

"Can I borrow your grease pencil?" the first man asked, and he rapidly sketched a new weapon on the back of the shield. "There's the handle, a chain about as long as my forearm, and then the metal ball with spikes."

The Frunge was clearly perplexed as he studied the drawing. "Are you sure it's supposed to look like this?"

"They were really common, at least on playing cards. Hey, do you have that library book with you, Geoff?"

"I think it's still in my pack," the other game designer said. He slid the strap off his shoulder, unsnapped the flap, and rummaged around inside. "Here you go."

The team leader flipped through the pages and quickly located several color photographs showing examples of the war flail he was talking about. If anything, Razood appeared even more puzzled than before.

"But these couldn't possibly have functioned as weapons," the blacksmith said slowly. "There's no way to control the heavy iron ball on the chain. You're more likely to injure yourself or your shield-mate with one of those spikes than to hit an enemy with it."

"But the pictures are from a museum collection," Geoff protested.

"What does the description say, Bill? I can read Humanese, but that font is a bit strange."

"Replica war flails of various types," the apprentice read.

"Check the descriptions of other pictures in the book."

Bill began skimming through the surrounding pages, reporting on the captions as he went. "Most of the photographs give a place and date where they think the weapon was manufactured, and some of the fancier pieces are identified as dress armor or gifts that were never intended for use in combat. And here's a suit of armor that was assembled from multiple sources, but those spiked ball things are the only ones listed as replicas."

"Just as I thought," Razood told the Bitters. "Some artist must have decided that a spiked ball on a chain would make a fine weapon to add to a painting, but I doubt they ever saw a battlefield."

"Are you sure?" the team leader asked doubtfully. "They're in a lot of games. Could you make one? I can pay three hundred creds for the mace and a spiked war flail."

"It would be more practical with a long handle and just enough chain to let the business end swing, maybe two links connected to a shorter shaft with spikes, rather than a heavy ball."

"That sounds like a weaponized version of an agricultural flail used by peasants," Geoff said. "There are pictures of what you just described in the book."

"The thing is, we're adding these weapons to the game by request," the team leader confessed. "The spiked ball flail was at the top of the list for the upgrade."

"I'll make one for you on two conditions," Razood offered. "First, you don't tell anybody where you got it. Second, if you need to map the ball in motion for the physics engine of your game, ask Flower to send a maintenance bot to swing the flail for you."

The two game designers exchanged a look. "We can live with that," Geoff said. "How long will it take you?"

"If you don't want a fancy handle, it's just a question of tapping an iron ball with holes and cutting some threads on small spikes to screw in. I have plenty of hand-forged chain around that I make for fun in my spare time. How heavy do you want the ball?"

"I guess if you could make it look like those replica pictures, that would be best," the team leader said. "Do we pay a deposit?"

"For a custom order like this that has no market value, I'll have to get the full amount upfront. But you can take the real mace with you today and I'll have the replica done by the end of your week."

After the game designers paid and departed, Bill asked, "How come you refused to forge cheap swords and axe heads for role-playing when I suggested it, but you're willing to make a completely imaginary weapon?"

"You just answered your own question."

"I did?"

"It's imaginary, nobody with any intelligence could possibly mistake it for real. My code prevents me from producing low-quality weapons that could actually find their way into combat."

"When's the last time the Frunge fought a war with medieval weapons?" Bill followed up.

"There was a period in our history when we had a number of tech ban worlds, like the Vergallians, and you never know when some enemy will deploy superior technology that prevents your modern weapons from working," Razood said. "Muscle-powered weapons practice remains a large part of basic training for our military and reserves. Don't you need to get going?"

"I'm supposed to help Harry in the cafeteria today, but he probably doesn't have much for me to do if you want me to come back this afternoon."

"This job will only take me a few hours and I don't want you learning bad habits. I'm going to start by visiting the booth in the bazaar where they sell those antique firearms and check if they have a small iron ball I can use rather than making one from scratch. Say hello to Jorb for me, and maybe I'll see you at supper."

"I'll be there serving," Bill promised, and headed off for his martial arts lesson at the Drazen's dojo. A couple of new students from Bits were there, and Julie arrived just on time, so Bill didn't get a chance to talk with her until after the session. Jorb beat him to the punch.

"How are you progressing at singing?" the Drazen asked Julie.

"I have to thank you for that. Rinka is a sweetheart, and I'm having a great time."

"You sound better already, and I noticed that your breathing has improved as well, but I meant, are you making progress about me?"

"We haven't really discussed you," Julie said. "I'm working my way around to it."

"I'm sure she knows I sent you, but she's too refined to say anything," Jorb said. "We need to come up with a plan to meet by accident in a public space with chaperones."

"How is it an accident if you make a plan?"

The Drazen groaned and pulled on his tentacle. "Just come up with a place to take her some evening and she'll know how to act. Bill will come with me, we'll meet, and you'll introduce us."

"Like a club?" Bill asked, suddenly worried about his role. "I don't know how to dance or anything."

"Not a club, it can't be a place with drinks. The ag decks are too wide open and there may not be enough people around, and restaurants are out for first meetings because of the whole food thing."

"What whole food thing?" Julie asked.

"You know, domestic implications and all that."

"Why does it have to be so complicated?" Bill asked.

"Talk to Razood if you want to hear about complicated courtships," Jorb said. "The Frunge are the worst on the tunnel network. They can spend years in contract negotiations before holding hands."

"How about game night at the library?" Julie suggested.

"Role-playing games?" the Drazen asked suspiciously. "It wouldn't be appropriate."

"We have a collection of old board games from Earth, especially ones that build your vocabulary or knowledge."

"Wordplay is perfect. When's game night?"

"Next Thursday."

"That far off?" Jorb complained. "Alright, it will give me a chance to come up with a song, just in case she asks. Sorry, but I've got to run now if I want to be early for my gig getting beat up by teenage girls at the finishing school."

"Did you understand half of that?" Bill asked Julie as they headed for the lift tube.

"Not really," the girl admitted. "It's funny when you think about it. The thing that reminds me that Jorb and Rinka are aliens isn't their tentacles, it's their conversation, and that's with my implant giving me perfect translations."

"Home," Bill told the lift tube capsule, which obligingly set off without seeking clarification. "I'm going to take a long shower and maybe even a short nap before I go in to work at the cafeteria. What's the rest of your day like?"

"Shower, diner, singing practice, theatre. I have to check with Flower three times a day just to figure out where I'm supposed to be. I'm beginning to envy people with full-time jobs."

"Can you believe the director has us standing in for cartoon characters?"

"Anime," Flower said over their implants as the two exited the lift tube capsule on their residential deck.

"I still don't get why it's necessary," Bill said stubbornly. "It's going to be embarrassing to have the director and the writers telling us to move around and pretend to be doing stuff."

"Between you and me, the director insists on calling you stand-ins because he's worked in a union environment where the only other option would be to call you principal animation actors."

"What's the difference?" Julie asked.

"About fifty creds an hour, plus residuals when the production is broadcast or copied through legitimate means," the Dollnick AI explained. "We'll only be using your vector representation for scaffolding."

"What does that mean?"

"It saves a great deal of computational time to capture your motion in blank form for the animation artists to dress up. Think of yourselves as living mannequins."

"So now you're saying we're going to have to act out the whole cartoon but we aren't going to get credit?"

"Anime, the term applies to both the characters and the finished animation, and no, you aren't going to have to act out every last movement."

"She just qualified my statement," Julie said, poking Bill in the shoulder. "Is she talking over your implant too? Whenever Flower starts using precise language like that it means she's putting something over on me."

"I guess we'll find out when the time comes," Bill said fatalistically, swiping his palm to open the door to his cabin. "Hey, do you want to grab a coffee or something after standing in tonight?"

"I'll probably be too tired, but we'll see."

"Be persistent," Flower advised Bill after the girl entered her own cabin. "She won't know that you're serious otherwise."

"I already feel like I'm stalking her," the young man grumbled as he headed for the bathroom. After a quick shower, he collapsed in bed for a nap. It felt like he had just fallen asleep when the Dollnick AI woke him for work. Ten minutes later, he found himself hand-mixing a bowl of something with the consistency of wet cement, while Harry thumbed through the printed version of the All Species Cookbook that the beetle doctor had brought from Union Station.

"Looks like it's stiffening up nicely," the baker said. "Does the spoon stand on its own if you leave it upright?"

"It's getting the spoon to move at all that's the problem," Bill complained. "What is this stuff?"

"I'm making a Verlock Ash Dough recipe I got from Flower using the suggested substitution from the All Species Cookbook of whole wheat for pumice. I can't believe they eat that stuff."

"Whole wheat?"

"Pumice. Whole wheat is good for you."

"But why are you using Earth ingredients to bake for aliens?"

"Because they can all digest it. I've been a baker my whole life, and I can tell you that the whole point of dessert is to give the diners something to look forward to at the end of the meal. Before the All Species Cookbook came out, all I could offer them was fruit every night."

"We have lots of fruit and I don't want to dry it all," Flower reminded him.

Harry poked the rapidly hardening mixture with his finger. "The aliens can all tolerate most of the basic foodstuffs from Earth, so if I can come up with something that looks and tastes a bit like their favorite desserts from back home using our ingredients, that will solve the problem."

"Not with Razood," Bill pointed out. "He doesn't eat grains."

177

"I thought I'd start with the low hanging fruit and come up with something for Brynlan. I'm suspicious Verlocks care more about the texture than the taste."

"So what do you want me to do with this?"

"Roll it out before it hardens. Try for a single sheet about as thick as your finger, and then cut it into squares and put them on the greased tray there. A half-hour in the oven should do for the first baking."

"Got it," Bill said, digging out the dough with both hands and plopping it on the counter for rolling. "At least it's sticking together."

"I wouldn't mind making different desserts for each species, but Flower thinks it's important that they share some part of the meal for the sake of camaraderie, and she doesn't count drinks."

"Don't you think it's weird that all of the aliens are affected by alcohol?"

Harry shrugged. "I'm not sure they are, at least, not in the same way. The Dollnicks are the only ones I've seen get tipsy at meals, but that may be because they only drink on special occasions."

"The Frunge and the Drazens imbibe more alcohol per capita than the other tunnel network species, though Humans aren't far behind," Flower interjected.

"So the Verlocks and the Grenouthians aren't drinkers?"

"They have greater body mass, higher alcohol tolerance, and don't make cultural allowances for drunks."

"Are these all right?" Bill asked, showing Harry the tray of raw biscuits. "They sure don't look like desserts."

"We're basically making hardtack, so take one of those chopsticks from the utensils drawer and poke holes in a grid, say at about two fingers width. It's to help make sure they bake all the way through and dry better."

178

"Do I have to preheat the oven?"

"I already did. When they made ship's biscuits on Earth, they usually baked them multiple times or dried them in kilns. It's less an item of food than a convenient way to store flour, but the Verlock likes biting into things that would break our teeth."

"So how did sailors eat them?" Bill asked as he began poking the biscuits with a chopstick.

"Sometimes they wrapped their hardtack in cloth and beat it to get smaller pieces they could suck on, but soaking worked better. Soup, tea, even seawater, according to what I've read. Once you've finished and put the tray in the oven, come help me with tonight's main course."

"Which I shouldn't have let you talk me into," Flower commented.

"It will be fine," Harry said. "I've always dabbled in pizza. When you have an oven and dough, it's hard not to experiment."

"Don't forget about Razood," Bill said, joining the baker at the main counter after putting the tray in the oven. "And the setpoint temperature on the oven jumped a hundred degrees when I closed the door."

"That's how I voice-programmed it," Harry said. "Have you ever ordered a pizza with friends and asked for half with one topping and half with another?"

"I've never ordered a whole pizza in my life. Just slices."

"I had an idea for preparing an entrée the aliens can share. Basically, I'm going to make a couple of pizzas that are divided into quadrants, where the toppings on each one are intended for a specific species. Razood gets crustless."

"Crustless pizza? That would just be a melted glob of cheese and sauce with little bits of other stuff mixed in."

"Pretty much, but I asked third officer Lynx for advice since she served as a cultural attaché for years and has eaten at all sorts of alien banquets. She assured me that the Frunge on Union Station order crustless pizza from human restaurants all the time."

"How about Jorb?"

"The Drazens are the easiest aliens to please, I'm not even making special slices for him. He can pick what he wants and just add hot sauce."

"Brynlan?"

"For the Verlock, I'm using beef jerky and salt cod for toppings," Harry said. "They're in the bowl there, if you can dice them up for me."

"The Vergallian?"

"You can't go wrong with vegetables for the Vergallians or the Grenouthians, though now that you ask, I'm not sure about mushrooms. Flower?"

"The Vergallians will eat mushrooms, but the Grenouthians would be so offended they would probably declare war."

"Hold the 'shrooms," Harry repeated to himself.

Fifteen

"I hope Flower didn't put bugs in our food," Irene said nervously. "It is Dollnick night, if you've forgotten."

"Did you think I was dressing up for the lecture after the meal?" Harry fumbled with his necktie, trying to remember how to tie the knot. "I thought tying a tie was supposed to be like riding a bicycle, but I've completely forgotten how to do this."

"I think Flower will care more about our being on time than how we look."

"You're probably right," Harry said, crumpling up his necktie and tossing it on the bed. "I'll just wear the jacket and go with an open collar."

"I never understood why men would want to be choked with a silk noose while eating. You don't see women sacrificing comfort for fashion."

Harry bit his tongue as his wife of over forty years looked straight into his eyes, daring him to respond. It was only thanks to the high heels she was wearing that their eyes were even near the same level, and he had a hard time believing that her wire-reinforced undergarments were built for comfort. As they strolled to the common room, he couldn't help noticing that she kept a grip on his arm for balance, probably because she hadn't worn heels in years. It turned out that at least two-thirds of the cooperative's members had dressed for the occasion, but the dozen bots wearing ship's livery came as a complete surprise.

"Where's the food line?" Irene asked.

"Must be table service tonight," Harry surmised. "It looks like everybody else is here so we better sit." The couple quickly found places between Nancy and Dave at their usual table.

"Welcome to the first ethnic food night at Flower's Paradise," the Dollnick AI announced over the public address system. "Tonight I'll be serving recipes from the Galactic Free Press that were submitted by Humans living and working on Dollnick open worlds. I'm giving those of you with dietary restrictions the night off, and there are three entrées that everyone can choose from. I'm catering the after-party for the bocce ball league with the leftovers later and I'll tell them it's Modern Italian cuisine."

"This should be interesting," Nancy muttered to Jack under her breath, as a serving bot towing a floating cart arrived at their table.

"Good evening," the bot greeted them in oddly accented English that Flower must have copied from an old movie. "May I suggest you all start with a refreshing fruit salad?"

"That sounds safe," Nancy said, and then reworded her response after Jack nudged her and shook his head. "I meant, that sounds very nice."

The bot opened a chilled compartment in the food cart and removed a large stainless steel bowl with straight sides. "Just say when," it instructed Nancy, adding a ladleful to the bowl that was part of her place setting.

"That's fine," she said immediately, the ladle being sized for a Dollnick.

The bot worked its way around the table ladling fruit salad into all eight bowls, and then returned to float alongside the cart while they ate.

"Other than you making it, what's so Dollnick about fruit salad, Flower?" Dave asked.

"The green, red and orange color scheme, plus the precision knife work," Flower responded via the bot's speaker grille, giving the impression that it was suffering from multiple personality disorder. "The cantaloupe pieces, being orange, are cut as rhombic dodecahedrons, while the watermelon, as befitting red fruit, is served as perfect spheres. Can you tell me how the green pieces are shaped?"

"Pyramids," Nancy replied immediately. "I noticed right away, but I didn't want to say anything in case it's considered impolite."

"Dollnicks don't suffer from the thin skins so many other species display while eating," Flower said proudly. "The only unforgivable offense is to ask how much something costs."

"Do you mean in general, or related to the price of food?" Harry asked.

"Specifically the food being served. We, I mean, biological Dollnicks, see that as a veiled insult."

"Couldn't somebody be asking how much a melon costs to find out if they can afford it?"

"In that case, they would ask where the melon was purchased. Dollnicks use price queries to indicate quality issues. For example, passengers stranded on an interstellar liner might ask the crew, 'How much did you pay for the last engine overhaul?' It's considered very witty in those circumstances."

"It's very good, the fruit salad," Brenda said.

"Of course. Everything was picked earlier today on the ag decks. You couldn't find quality like this on Earth unless you lived on a farm, and maybe not then."

"Can I get another serving?" Dave asked.

"As healthy as fruit is, it's high in sugars and I'd rather you didn't," Flower said, and then the bot's voice shifted back to that of an English butler. "Your choices for the main course are spoon worms, Sheezle bug hash with gravy, and roast Furg with blended larvae sauce."

"Uh, could I just get a sandwich?"

"They aren't real Sheezle bugs or Furg," Flower said, taking control of the bot's speaker again. "Think of it as tribute food, like if I served you pistachio ice cream in the shape of a celery stalk."

"Oh, I'd like that. Then whatever is fine. I'll take the spoon worms."

"Very good, sir," the butler voice declared, and bringing a new stainless steel container out of the cart, began spooning fat, squirming worms onto Dave's plate. "Just say when."

"When! What is this? You just said we weren't getting real Dollnick food."

"And you aren't," the bot said, reverting to Flower's voice yet again. "Echiurus echiurus, better known as spoon worms, are the closest Humans can come to eating Dollnick Snakees. I maintain a saltwater tidal pool where I grow them as a treat for the captain. Spoon worms are a Korean delicacy."

"Could you keep them for the captain and I'll try the Sheezle bug hash?"

"Wait," Nancy said. "What's the hash made from, Flower?"

"Earth ingredients," the AI hedged.

"Are any of them alive?" Dave asked.

"Definitely not. And it's baked rather than fried, reducing the number of empty calories."

"You're the only one counting, but I'll try it."

"Would anybody else care for spoon worms?" the bot asked in its butler-voice. On receiving no reply, it tilted Dave's plate to slide the rejected entrée back into the stainless steel container, and then brought out a casserole dish with a glass lid. The bot removed the lid and began slicing squares of the baked hash.

"It smells heavenly," Irene said. "That's what I'll have as well."

"Me too," Jack chimed in, and all of the other diners at the table jumped on the safe option, rather than trying the as-of-yet unseen substitute for roast Furg with blended larvae sauce. The hash proved to be crunchier than expected, but it had a rich nutty flavor, and it matched well with the braised asparagus and fresh corn, which Jack explained was close to a staple crop he had grown for Dollnicks on their ag worlds.

"And now for dessert," the bot announced, after collecting the plates and bowls. "I give you, Weevil Mud."

"Is that what I think it is?" Dave asked, his eyes going wide.

"It looks like chocolate ice cream with chocolate chips!" Brenda exclaimed.

"The Dollnick original is oil-saturated peat with weevils, but the recipe called for substituting ice cream and raisins," Flower said. "I thought as long as we're getting crazy, I'd swap the raisins for chocolate chips, but don't expect to see it more than once a year."

While the cooperative members devoured their sinful dessert, the bots circulated with hot drinks and cleared away the other plates. Instead of the common room emptying out after the meal, a trickle of non-members arrived, including Woojin, Lynx, and Dianne. A few people began pointing towards the back of the room, and there Harry spotted a number of the aliens from his cafeteria, who had slipped in through a side entrance. The beetle doctor came in through the front, glared at Dave through multi-faceted eyes, and then joined the other aliens.

"Do you think he knows I had two servings of ice cream?" Dave asked guiltily.

"Wipe the corner of your mouth," Brenda whispered.

Jack rose from his spot and walked over to the small lectern that a bot had placed where the steam table was usually located. The large display panel behind him that most often showed an exterior view of the colony ship and had recently been given over to recordings of various legacy games, now displayed a title card that read, "The Business of EarthCent is Business."

"I'd like to welcome everybody to the maiden lecture of our series, but first, let me thank Flower for the wonderful meal," Jack said, and then allowed time for the enthusiastic applause. "Our guest tonight will be Third Officer Pyun Lynx, and she'll be speaking about EarthCent's mission to do its best for humanity. Lynx worked as an independent trader for ten years before being recruited by EarthCent Intelligence and eventually serving as the cultural attaché on Union Station. If you didn't pick up on the name, Lynx is married to our captain, Pyun Woojin, and they have a lovely daughter, Em, who is home sleeping after an exhausting day at nursery school. Mrs. Pyun?"

"Thank you, Jack," Lynx said, stepping up to the lectern. "Although I have served as a diplomat, I never really cared for making speeches, so please feel free to interrupt at any time with questions and maybe we can have a group discussion. If any of you are afraid of slide shows, don't worry, this is the only one I have prepared," she continued, making a sweeping gesture to indicate the display panel behind her. "It's from an address that the President of EarthCent gave to a recent graduating class from our diplomacy school. Does anybody recognize the quote?"

"The chief business of the American people is business," Nancy spoke up. "President Calvin Coolidge, though he's usually misquoted in the form you're showing."

"Hmm, I think our president's version is snappier," Lynx said. "When the Stryx opened Earth and established EarthCent as the sole contact point for official dealings between our people and the tunnel network, they didn't give our diplomats many guidelines as to what would be expected of them. For the first fifty or so years of EarthCent's existence, our ambassadors were tolerated by the tunnel network members, but our people were seen as little more than the latest source of unskilled labor for species that avoid using automation whenever possible."

The audience began to point in Lynx's direction and make appreciative noises. It took the captain's wife a few seconds to realize that Flower had started showing still images on the display panel illustrating the different types of manual labor done by humans around the tunnel network.

"Er, thank you, Flower," Lynx continued. "Our ambassadors did their best to represent humanity through official channels, such as serving on the committees mandated by the Stryx on their stations, but progress was slow because the aliens saw, and continue to see us, as primitives. How many people here have watched Grenouthian documentaries about Earth?"

Every hand in the room went up.

"And how many of you would say that those documentaries paint a positive picture of our progress?"

"The one about spectacular bridge collapses did end with a quick survey of famous suspension bridges that have been standing for over two centuries," somebody called out.

"That's true, but were you aware that ending was only added after the success of 'Let's Make Friends' on the Grenouthian network?"

"I guess I wasn't."

"What we've learned over the last couple of decades is that the business of the tunnel network is business. Until we had something more to offer the other species than our uneducated opinions, the aliens simply didn't find us that interesting."

"So EarthCent decided if we can't beat 'em, we'll join 'em," somebody else called out.

"I would put it a little differently, perhaps saying that humanity is finally growing up," Lynx said. "The Stryx have their own opaque reasons for doing what they do, but the biological species aren't out there scouring the galaxy for charity cases. There are over six billion humans working on alien worlds at this point, and while the majority are contract laborers, an increasing number are living on open worlds, where our communities are self-governing within the framework set up by host species. And EarthCent itself may one day be replaced by the Conference of Sovereign Human Communities."

"EarthCent recently gave us permission to open a research facility on Earth," the beetle doctor spoke up through his external translation box. "If the business of EarthCent is business, does that mean I'm welcome to manufacture pharmaceuticals here on Flower and sell them on Earth?"

"Earth doesn't have any trade barriers against imports, but there may well be regulations pertaining to medications. What kind of pharmaceuticals were you hoping to sell, M793qK?"

"Placebos. There shouldn't be any problem with safety since they're just colored sugar pills, and the profit margins are unbeatable."

"Uh, don't placebos only work if you tell people that they're real drugs?"

"Not according to the research I've done. Most visitors to my office leave with a prescription for a placebo, and I always describe exactly what they're getting. It's been a particular boon for my older patients who have difficulty keeping the complicated timing regimen for their previously prescribed Earth medications straight, and placebos eliminate the issue of drug interactions. I've been able to wean approximately half of my patients completely off their meds."

"Other than your placebos."

"Your people are too habituated to taking pills to stop abruptly," the alien doctor explained. "After I correct the underlying condition or assumption, I put them on a maintenance regime of placebos to prevent psychological withdrawal symptoms."

"What did he mean about underlying assumptions?" Dave whispered to Harry. "Is he saying that I was overmedicated?"

"You're better off not knowing," the baker replied.

"I have a hypothetical question about the preserved food business," Flower announced over the same public address system through which she was piping Lynx's lecture. "Say somebody wanted to start manufacturing pre-packaged desserts."

"Somebody like you?" the third officer asked.

"Well, yes. The release of the new All Species Cookbook has resulted in a sharp increase in demand for Earth's agricultural products. I already dedicate the majority of my agricultural capacity to growing your crops, but rather than selling in bulk and leaving most of the profit on the table, I want to target a few verticals where I can control the whole supply chain."

"So you want to grow the crops, process them into ingredients, cook the food, freeze it—"

"Vacuum pack," Flower interrupted. "One of the advantages of traveling through space is that you get the vacuum for free."

"Isn't it easy to keep frozen food in space as well?"

"You still have to remove the heat, and then it needs to be stored in the shade. And don't forget that refrigeration is required as soon as you send the food to market."

"I see. Why pre-packaged desserts?"

"High margins, plus I have the personnel in place. I'm especially interested in holiday desserts that can be prepared well in advance, such as fruitcakes and tinned cookies."

"Personnel—is that you?" Irene asked her husband.

"She's been hinting lately," Harry said. "Are you talking about me, Flower?"

"You do seem to have a gift for desserts," the Dollnick AI replied. "If there's one thing I've learned operating as a circuit ship, it's the importance of achieving scale. I was planning a packaged food business already, and adding desserts will help flesh out my offerings."

"You have bigger ambitions than taking over the galactic dessert market?" Lynx inquired.

"As soon as I can find the labor, I intend to start selling meal kits based on recipes from the All Species Cookbook. I'm counting on you to negotiate licensing terms with EarthCent so I don't have to evade the trademark, and I'm willing to pay a premium for a monopoly. I believe you know all of the individuals involved in the cookbook's production."

"You're springing this on me in the middle of a lecture?"

"You brought up business," Flower pointed out.

"If Lynx can't get them to agree, how would you go about evading the trademark?" Brenda asked, her legal curiosity aroused.

"While the phrase 'All Species Cookbook' is protected by the Stryx, it's a weak trademark in the sense that it's a literal description of the product using common words. If I have to publish the 'Every Species Cookbook' myself and base the meal kits on that, it will serve nearly the same purpose."

"Where would you get the recipes?" Harry asked.

"From the All Species Cookbook," Flower replied. "I'm not aware of any legal system that grants copyright protection for recipes, but I'd prefer to work with EarthCent on this."

"Soup kits would be interesting," the Grenouthian director said. "When I travelled with a theatrical company for fifty years, we rarely had time to prepare hot meals."

"Can I quote you on that?"

"I'll even say it on camera in return for the standard residual when the ad runs."

"And I suppose I should hire a Human attorney while I'm at it," Flower said. "Are you available, Brenda?"

"You mean paid work, on top of my volunteering?"

"Good point. We'll start with free and see how much of your time I require."

"Does anyone other than our Dollnick AI friend have a question?" Lynx inquired.

"I do," one of the three sisters who performed as the Barry Girls spoke up. "Is our independent living cooperative dependent on the success of these business ventures? Are we going to have to move again if Flower doesn't reach some level of profitability that nobody has told us about?"

"I can answer that," Jack said. "Flower has promised that she can maintain our facility even if she goes back to work for the Dollnicks as a colony ship, though the loss of the rest of the human population on board would obviously put a crimp in our recreational opportunities."

"Things have gotten a little more complicated," Flower admitted. "It turns out that my case is without precedent in Dollnick jurisprudence. Like most of our colony ships, my construction was financed by a number of families whose descendants lived on board and shared in my profits. When they abandoned ship, they gave up their financial interest, but when I started working towards reinstatement, they filed suit for a thousand years of missed payments, plus interest. It's basically a tactical move on the part of the heirs, an attempt to blackmail me into paying them to go away so I can proceed with my case."

"A thousand years of compound interest?" Lynx exclaimed. "Would that leave you broke?"

"Deeply in debt, though I've appealed the ruling. The courts have frozen my accounts in Dollnick space, but fortunately, I do most of my banking with the Stryx."

Sixteen

"I don't mind helping Bill with a delivery, but why didn't you just send a bot to carry this thing?" Julie asked out loud.

"I've learned that presentation counts and that my bots aren't appropriate in all circumstances," Flower responded. "It's just down the corridor on the left."

"Is that Bill waiting? I can't see his face with that giant thing he's carrying. What is it?"

"A fruit basket."

"Are you really growing enough fruit trees to supply five million people?"

"I might have been overly optimistic in my population projections."

"Hey, Julie," Bill said. "I hope that thing isn't as heavy as it looks."

"It barely weighs anything at all," the girl said. She let the end of the large cylindrical package fall to the deck and gestured at the door where he had been waiting for her. "Is this the place?"

"Unwrap the present before you go in," Flower instructed Julie. "The plastic bag can be recycled later."

"Let me do that," Bill said, setting down the giant fruit basket and carefully slitting the sealed bag at one end with his pocket knife. He pulled out a giant stuffed cylinder that was too large to be practical as a pillow. "What is it?"

"Me," Flower said. "Can't you see the bay doors on the end?"

"I wondered why I was making a pickup at a toy store," Julie said. "It really is a stuffed colony ship."

"I'm trying to standardize on a gift package for new arrivals. Remember, you're here as my welcoming delegation. If you can't come up with anything to say, I'll prompt you over your implants."

"But when we were rehearsing Shakespeare for the Grenouthian, you said that prompting was a bad idea," Julie protested.

"That was different because you had a script to memorize. We'll just play this by ear."

Bill picked up the fruit basket and pressed the door pad. "Delivery," he announced.

"Come in," a woman's voice replied, and the door slid open.

Julie and Bill entered the cabin, where a young woman was sitting in an overstuffed chair with a tiny infant in her arms.

"We're the welcoming committee," Bill said, standing awkwardly with the giant fruit basket. "Did you just join us at the galactic heritage site?"

"Me? I've been on board for three years, but this one arrived two days ago," the young woman said, turning a little to show off the sleeping infant's tiny face. "I'm Sue, and this is Dawn."

"What a pretty name," Julie said. "He's Bill and I'm Julie. I guess this stuffed colony ship is for Dawn."

"I think it's a little big for her right now. Maybe in another year or two?"

"The fruit must be for you," Bill said, setting the basket on the table.

"Fruit is healthy for nursing mothers," Flower prompted over his implant.

"Fruit is healthy for nursing mothers," Bill repeated, and then turned red when both women looked at him oddly. "Flower made me say that."

"Oh, she's been giving me advice nonstop ever since I got pregnant," Sue told them. "I didn't think I was ready for a baby, and the father jumped ship as soon as I told him. Flower offered to be the godmother, and she promised free daycare when my maternity leave is up."

"Did you just change cabins?" Julie asked. "Everything looks brand new."

"Flower insisted that I spend two weeks in her maternity corridor, just to get away from it all and bond with Dawn. I guess it's a Dollnick tradition, and it's nice being able to meet other first-time mothers. Come in," she added, when a new visitor announced herself.

The door slid open and another young woman with an infant in her arms entered. Julie nudged Bill, and they made their excuses and left the two mothers together to enjoy the fruit.

"You set up a maternity ward, Flower?" Julie asked.

"Dollnicks traditionally encourage new mothers to nest together for several cycles. There aren't enough births on board yet for a full-fledged maternity garden, and your married women return home too early, but I'm hoping that will change. I have one more task for the two of you before your stand-in work."

"What's that?" Bill asked.

"I want your impressions of a new decorating scheme for cabins."

"Why us?" Julie asked suspiciously.

"If I explain first, I won't get your natural reaction. It's just down the corridor on the way to the lift tube. I'll open the door."

"Since when do you ask for our advice?"

"Don't I always ask for your input before making decisions that impact your lives?"

"Not that I've noticed. If you do ask my opinion, you just ignore it anyway."

"I like to think that I give Humans a vote but not a veto," Flower explained. "There, the cabin on the left. Go right in."

"It's very pink," Bill said uncertainly, halting just inside the doorway.

"If I were six years old I'd think you just made me a princess," Julie said. "What's it supposed to be?"

"A bridal suite," Flower said. "I project solid growth in my business catering to retirees, but what I really need to make my long term population goals is natural increase. Doesn't the décor make you want to procreate? Try the bed."

"Send a bot to try the bed. I'm going to the theatre."

"Wait up," Bill called after Julie as she stomped out of the cabin. "I didn't have anything to do with that."

"I know. I think Flower's legal problems are making her a little nuts."

"A little more nuts."

"I can hear you," the Dollnick AI commented.

"Stop trying to push us around, Flower. It's embarrassing," Bill said. "Isn't this why your original crew abandoned you in the first place?"

"Their main complaint was that rather than arguing over their choice of destination, I tricked them into believing

I was following instructions and made a better choice for them."

"They colonized the wrong world?"

"The right world, just not the one they chose. It was a great success. Don't you think I make good decisions, Julie?"

"I'm not talking to you."

Other than a few aliens on stage, the theatre was empty when the pair arrived. Bill found his shovel in the props box, while Razood handed Julie her tray and coffee pot. The Farling doctor was just demonstrating how he could create a powerful gust of wind with his wings, knocking Jorb off his feet. The martial artist managed to convert his momentum into a roll, all of which was captured by the circle of floating immersive cameras.

"You're really the complete package," the Grenouthian director said to M793qK in admiration. "Maybe we should make you the superhero and the rest of us could be villains."

"The writers would revolt," Flower said. "Have you captured enough of our good doctor's motions for the animators to get started?"

"Whether you have or haven't, I'm almost late for an appointment," the beetle rubbed out on his speaking legs. "Somebody owes me a big basket of strawberries."

"I had a bot drop them off at your clinic."

M793qK disappeared backstage and the director pointed at Julie and Bill. "All right, the two of you are up next. Let's see if you can decapitate anybody, Julie."

"You want me to do what?" the girl asked.

"Throw the tray. Your character, Refill, is an expert with improvised weapons, including hot liquids and table utensils. The tray can be deployed on either offense or defense."

"Send it my way," Jorb offered. "I'll catch it."

"This is crazy," the girl said, but she flung the tray in the Drazen's general direction. It curved wildly and skipped off the stage before being snagged by Lume with one of his lower arms.

"Hey, that was kind of like a Frisbee," Bill observed. "Maybe if you held it with the rim down and flicked it off your forefinger it would fly straight."

"I never learned to play Frisbee," Julie said. "And it doesn't seem like much of a weapon."

"The animators will add rotating blades that pop out in flight," the Grenouthian told her.

"So how is it an improvised weapon?"

"It's entertainment, it doesn't have to make sense. And who are you?" the director demanded of a figure who waddled onto the stage. The latecomer was wearing a floor-length overcoat with a row of false appendages fashioned from coat hangers running down each side.

"Dave. I'm standing in for M793qK."

"You can't stand in for a stand-in."

"Doc said he's going to be too busy for storyboarding but he'll show up when you need him for vector mapping," Dave explained. "He's paying me."

"Farling prima donna," the Grenouthian grumbled. "There's one in every production."

"So what are we doing today?" Harry asked.

"Our goal was to see the characters interacting with each other and the villain to get an idea of possible match-ups, but I don't see how Pillowcase Man helps with that. I set up the cameras to begin some basic motion capture for scaffolding moves today, and I'll send the results to the writers so they can get started on dialogue."

"Don't you need to have a story first?"

"We've got a back story, and that's just as important. An unidentified colony ship is transporting the survivors of a peaceful galaxy that's been overrun by aggressive aliens. Flower and I have discussed the objectives in depth, and we're looking for humor and pathos."

"And action," Razood said, twirling his heavy hammer.

"And action, with a little mystery, a dash of romance, and plenty of suspense," the director summed up. "It's a pretty standard setup, and the writers estimated it will take a month to produce a full script for the first episode, with drafts for the next six to maintain the continuity."

"I ordered the standard twenty episode package up-front," Flower informed them.

"Right, but the writers won't plot past six until we see how the premiere does," the director said. "If the first episode bombs, they can kill off all of the heroes and make it a supervillain story."

"Does that mean more work for me?" Dave asked.

The Grenouthian pointedly ignored the Farling's stand-in and turned to the Verlock. "Why don't you start us off with some basic scaffolding, Slomo?"

"What's basic scaffolding?" Julie asked.

"Motion capture for standard sequences, like running down a corridor or getting in or out of a lift tube. Once we have those in the can, the animators will be able to use them over and over again as the plot requires."

"So we're going to have to go out and run around the corridors in these costumes?"

"No need," the director said. "Flower has a nearly un-limited library of stock imaging from the ship's interior.

We just need to capture each of you in motion and run a filter to remove the background. Then we'll slap your hologram into Flower's stock imaging and the animators will take it from there. "Brynlan?"

The Verlock offered the bunny a facetious salute, and then began sprinting across the stage at his top speed, which was regular walking pace for most bipedal species in the same height range.

"Good, good," the Grenouthian said, peering at the viewfinder of the nearest floating camera. "You must be working out. Now come back at your regular speed."

The bulky alien ambled back at a pace that would have left a three-toed sloth behind but would have lost to most species of giant turtle.

"Perfect. How about some of those balancing exercises I've seen Verlocks do. We can pass them off as martial arts training."

"You're really trying to make me sweat," Grynlan said, but he slowly raised his arms over his head while shifting his weight to one leg and bringing the other off the floor behind him. Then he reached back with one hand to grasp his foot while leaning forward and sticking the other hand way out in front.

"I can't believe the Verlock is more flexible than I am," Julie whispered to Bill behind her hand. "I couldn't do that in a million years."

"You could be doing it by the end of the week if you'd start the yoga regimen I suggested rather than sticking to the minimum stretches," Flower scolded over the girl's implant.

"Great," the director declared. "Take a break, Brynlan, and let's see what you can do, Lume."

The Dollnick launched into a tumbling run, flipping from his feet to his upper hands three times before leaping high in the air and coming down with all four of his arms stretched behind his back, creating twin V's.

"Way to stick the landing," the director complimented him. "I'm beginning to think that you're wasted as a mastermind."

"He could be our secret weapon," Jorb suggested. "I can imagine a scene where the villain and his minions have captured us all, but they don't pay attention to Thinker because of his reputation as an armchair hero. You'll have to put something in his back story about being a former assassin."

"Why former?" the Vergallian schoolmistress asked, struggling to adjust her halter top. "And if I get my hands on the artist who thought it made sense for a superhero to run around in this sorry excuse for a bra, I'm going to kill him."

"Them," Flower said. "Your Battle Royale char was created by a team of young men."

"Figures," Avisia scoffed. "Just for the record, I refuse to jump wearing this thing."

"Julie, Bill. Let's have some slow dancing," the Grenouthian ordered.

"Wouldn't it make more sense for Brynlan to do all of the slow stuff?" Bill asked.

The director pinched his nose between a furry thumb and forefinger. "Not dancing slowly, slow dancing. Arms around each other, cheek to cheek. The main reason I cast the two of you is so we could have a romantic interest."

"I've never slow danced," the young man mumbled.

"Julie, you teach him."

"I've never slow danced either," Julie admitted.

"What a species!" the Grenouthian groaned. "New homework, the two of you. Learn how to slow dance."

"Did Flower put you up to this?"

"Look, we need a romance interest and Harry is too old for you. I'm not fooling around with cross-species nonsense or we'll get stuck with an 'Adults Only' rating, so the two of you are it."

"Is adult anime even a thing?" Dave asked.

"Unfortunately, but it's not a direction that either Flower or myself are willing to go. If I wanted to produce pornography, I would have taken the job on Timble."

"They wanted you to direct sex documentaries?" Harry asked in disbelief.

"That's right," the Grenouthian said angrily. "They said it's an underserved market and the sky is the limit. The only reason they asked me to the interview was because of my experience with Humans and the fact that none of their studio directors were willing to take the job. I told them where they could stuff their guaranteed salary and ten points in the production."

"So why did you and Flower decide on making superhero anime that you don't even have a plot for yet rather than doing something more conventional."

"What we're doing is conventional," Flower said. "My preference would have been educational anime for children, but it's a tough market to break into, and I don't know if I could have gotten so many of the Bitters to participate. I'm trying to manage an economy here, if you haven't noticed."

Seventeen

"I'm nervous," Rinka confessed, as she followed Julie into the library. "Are there any other Drazens here? Maybe I should go home."

"We're early," Julie reassured her. "I like the white ribbon."

"This?" the Drazen asked, extending her tentacle, which was wrapped in a white spiral like a barber's pole. "You don't think it's too dressy?"

"Not at all. Do you have a preference for which game we play?"

"I wouldn't know any of them. Are they all two-player games?"

"Most of them are flexible, though some have a maximum of four players, like Scrabble."

"Scrabble, I like the sound of that," Rinka said, and then began singing softly to herself.

Julie was starting to worry that the Drazen girl would panic when Bill showed up with Jorb in tow. She took a Scrabble box from the game stand Dewey had set up and led the way to one of the small tables with four folding chairs.

"Oh, here comes Bill," Julie said. Her voice sounded so unnatural to her own ears that she felt a sudden sympathy for the Grenouthian director's earlier attempts to teach her acting. "It looks like he has our friend Jorb with him."

Rinka grabbed Julie's forearm below the table and whispered fiercely, "You can't leave me alone with him."

"Of course not," Julie said, and called to the newcomers. "Hey, guys. We were about to play Scrabble. Want to join us?"

"I would be honored," Jorb replied formally, taking the chair opposite Rinka's. "You're the choir mistress who presented to Flower's student selection committee on Union Station," he continued, speaking directly to the Drazen girl. "I've heard wonderful things about your work here."

"Thank you," Rinka replied in a voice so low that the humans could hardly hear her. "Julie told me that you and she are friends and neighbors, Bill. It must be nice to have somebody so close you can talk to."

"We mainly see each other at the dojo or theatre practice, though these days we're just standing in for anime," Bill said. "Has anybody played this game before?"

"I have," Julie said, "with my teacher bot. I've never had to keep score, though. The rules are on the inside of the cover."

"Let me see that," Jorb said, as if he were claiming the wine list in a restaurant, and ran his eyes down the dense text. "Looks pretty straightforward, with points on the tiles and multipliers on the board. We all pick a tile to set the order of turns, and whoever goes first gets a double word score."

"You can read English?"

"I picked it up studying your martial arts manuals. We used to get some Humans at the dojo on Union Station and I wanted to understand their fighting styles."

"My spelling is pretty terrible," Bill said. "Maybe we could do teams. How's your English, Rinka?"

"I learned to read it for a course I took at the Open University and my students here all speak Humanese. I only activate my implant if I don't understand something."

"Why don't we play Humans versus Drazens," Jorb suggested, giving the felt bag holding the wooden tiles a shake. "The ladies can pick a letter to see which team goes first."

"I hate going first because there are no words to build off," Julie said. She put her hand in the bag and pulled out a letter. "P."

"L," the Drazen girl declared, showing her own tile. "Now what?"

"Put your letters back, I'll shake up the bag, then we each take seven letters in the order we'll be playing," Jorb told her. "Everybody take a rack to hold the letters."

The bag made the round of players as they all populated their racks, and then Rinka asked, "Do I have to use up all seven letters?"

"No, it's really hard. I only managed it a few times playing my teacher bot," Julie replied.

"And how about the teacher bot?" Jorb asked.

"It played down to my level, I guess. All the games worked that way."

"I'm not sure about the spelling, but I remember the instrument," Rinka said, and began laying out letters. "Z, I, T, H, E, R, S."

"What are they?" Bill asked.

"Stringed instruments with a flat sounding-box," the Drazen girl explained. "Is it a good word?"

"Move the 'Z' onto the double letter," Jorb advised her. "Let's see. That's twenty and nine, times two for going first, plus fifty for using up all of your letters. One hundred and eight for Team Drazen."

"I can't believe you used up all of your letters," Julie said, studying her own rack.

"Beginners luck," Rinka told her, drawing seven new tiles from the bag.

"Sorry I'm taking so long. I just—there. D, O, N, U, T," she declared, pluralizing the word with the 'S' of ZITHERS.

"Triple letter on the 'U,'" Jorb congratulated her. "That's nine for Team Human. Are we playing you have to use words related to our professions? I have, T, R, A, I, N, I, N, G."

"We're dead," Bill groaned.

"Nine, double for eighteen, plus fifty," the scorekeeper said. "That's a hundred and seventy-six for Team Drazen. You're up, Bill."

"See how he used the 'I' that Rinka put down in the middle of his word?" Julie said to Bill.

"There's no 'I' in couple," the Drazen girl recited, causing Jorb to wince.

"I thought there was no 'I' in team," Bill countered, studying his letters. "Anyway, I only have one vowel and it's a 'U'. Sorry, Julie, but this is all I can come up with. F, O, U, R."

"You got a double word," Jorb said. "Fourteen and nine makes twenty-three for Team Human. Speaking of doubles, isn't two always better than one?" he added, risking a quick smile at the Drazen girl.

"You sound like Flower," Julie said, arranging and rearranging her tiles on the rack. "I think her goal is to fill every cabin on the ship with a family to maximize the number of people on board."

"Is it me again already?" Rinka asked. "I have T, O, G, E, T, H, E, R."

"Triple letter on the 'E' and the 'R,'" Jorb said. "That's sixteen plus fifty, Drazens have two hundred and thirty-two."

"Don't you have to write anything down?" Bill asked.

"It's just a few small numbers. My memory isn't that bad."

"H, A, L, V, E, D," Julie declared, making the word with the 'H' in TOGETHER so it reached the triple word score at the bottom.

"Are you sure that's how it's spelled?" Bill asked doubtfully. "I thought it was with an 'F.'"

"You're thinking of the other half," Rinka told him. "Halve means to cleave something in twain."

"To what?"

"Forty-two," Jorb reported. "The 'L' was on a double letter, so Team Human is up to sixty-five. I have C, O, U, R, T, I, N, G," he continued without a pause, building the word around the 'T' he had previously put down for TRAINING. "That's twelve times two plus fifty—three hundred and six for us."

"I never even reached two hundred playing with the teacher bot," Julie commented.

"Together, courting," Flower said in Bill's head. "You could learn something from your friends. Do you want my help?"

"I want a seven-letter word," Bill tried to subvoc, but it came out like a whisper, causing the other players to look at him oddly.

"I meant do you want help with Julie," the Dollnick AI replied. "I have lots of ideas."

"Is there a time limit?" Bill asked, looking back and forth between his rack and the board. "I have some words, but I want to get the most points."

208

"I've never played so fast in my life," Julie said.

"Your teacher bot didn't go immediately after you did?" Rinka asked.

"It always took the exact same amount of time as I used with all the games we played. I don't know if it was just being polite or if it was trying to teach me a lesson."

"J, U, G," Bill announced, taking the triple word score opened by the 'G' in COURTING.

"Thirty-nine," Jorb said. "That's a hundred and four already for Team Human. Has it ever occurred to anybody that this game would be a great way to exchange secret messages?"

"What do you mean?" Julie asked.

"You know, like Bill could put down, T, O, N, I, G, H, T, and you could reply, A, N, Y, T, I, M, E."

"How could you do that?" Bill demanded.

"Sorry, I was just teasing," the Drazen apologized. "I thought it was pretty obvious that you like her. I didn't mean to embarrass anybody."

"What?" Bill's face turned red, and he sputtered, "I meant, how could you come up with two seven-letter-words without even thinking?"

"I wasn't counting," Jorb said. "I guess I'm sort of locked in."

"P, A, R, E, N, T, A, L," Rinka announced, emptying her rack for the third straight time. "I used your 'L,'" she added to Julie.

"Double 'P' plus double word makes twenty-six plus fifty for using up your letters," Jorb reported. "Three hundred and eighty-two."

"Don't rush," Bill said to Julie as she started laying out tiles.

"I mainly have vowels and I need to use them up," the girl replied. "I'm not going to get a seven-letter word so I'm hoping to pick up some letters with points. P, E, E, L."

"You and Bill are getting all of the triple words," Rinka observed.

"That's because you and Jorb don't need them."

"Eighteen, and you're up to a hundred and twenty-two," Jorb calculated. "I can use a triple if you want. I have D, O, L, L, N, I, C, K. That's sixteen times three is forty-eight, plus fifty, gives us four hundred and eighty."

"Dollnick?" the Drazen girl asked in disbelief.

"I'll take it back," Jorb offered, belatedly recognizing that he had ruined the subtext of his word exchange with Rinka for the sake of scoring points. Bill grabbed his wrist and stopped him.

"It's better you keep putting down big words because it will put us out of our misery quicker."

"But I just remembered from the instructions that Dollnick is a proper name so I can't use it," Jorb protested.

"It's also a noun," Flower interjected over their implants. "Plus, it's my ship and I say it's a word."

"I think I have to powder my nose," Rinka said, rising from her chair. "Coming?"

Julie took a second to figure out that the Drazen girl was talking to her. "Oh, right. Me too. We'll be right back."

As soon as they were out of sight, Jorb wrapped his tentacle around his face to cover his eyes so he wouldn't have to look at the Scrabble board.

"What's wrong?" Bill asked.

"You heard her," the distraught lover replied. "She wants to powder her nose."

"I guessed that was just something Drazen girls say when they have to use the bathroom."

"Is that how it works with Humans? With us, it means she smelled something she didn't like and she wants to desensitize her olfactory organ. We have a special powder for that."

"You're saying she thinks we smell?"

"It's figurative, not literal. Why did I have to put down DOLLNICK? You saw that she got upset right afterwards."

"She was upset?"

"It was going so well," Jorb continued. "First we got all that career talk out of the way, then she put down TOGETHER to let me know she's considering my suit. I put down COURTING so she'd know that I'm serious, and she put down PARENTAL to remind me that her family isn't on board. Then what did I do? What did I do?" Jorb repeated.

"You put down DOLLNICK."

"I put down DOLLNICK! What was I thinking?"

"If I had your letters, I would have put it down if I'd seen it."

"Thank you," Flower said over Bill's implant.

"But we were having an intimate conversation and now she must think that I'm nuts. DOLLNICK? What's she supposed to make of that?"

Rinka stopped and grabbed Julie's arm before they made it to the bathroom. "DOLLNICK?" the Drazen girl repeated. "What's that supposed to mean? Does he think that Flower can fill in for my parental guidance?"

"I don't see why not," Flower commented in Julie's head.

"I was relieved that we got all of that career stuff out of the way so quickly, and when he put down COURTING, well, I don't have to tell you that my heart skipped a beat. But DOLLNICK?"

"He used up all seven letters," Julie pointed out. "What was he supposed to put down?"

"It's not about the score," Rinka said. "I'm worried that he's too competitive."

"Give him another chance and I'm sure he'll come up with something sweet. You put down all seven-letter words too."

"But I didn't put down DOLLNICK."

"She probably thinks I'm too competitive now," Jorb said to Bill. "You have to help me out and get some points."

"I'm trying. It's just that I'm not a big reader and I've never been that good at spelling. I don't get how you do it."

"Games like this are probably easier for non-native speakers with good memories. It's just a big puzzle for me. Look," the Drazen said, reaching across the table and turning Bill's rack sideways so they could both see it. "You've got a blank and an 'S'. That's a perfect setup."

"I thought the blank was like a penalty tile I couldn't use. I've had it all game."

"No, you should have asked. It can be anything you want. And you've got an 'X', that's worth a lot of points."

"I can't think of any 'X' words."

"Can't think of any—there must be millions of them. And 'C' from COURTING is a great open space because you'll get the triple word. Look, you have 'ING' too. COAXINGS."

"Is that a word?"

"Do I have to coax you to put it down?"

"Very funny. But plural?"

212

"Why not?" Jorb turned the rack back to Bill. "If you can find something better, put it down, but COAXINGS is worth a hundred and four points."

"But Julie will know that I'm cheating."

"You're not cheating, I'm cheating. Help a friend."

"Listen to the Drazen," Flower advised over Bill's implant.

"Did you miss us?" Julie asked as the girls returned.

"I did," Bill said, and the tips of his ears turned bright red. "I mean, I have a good word. C, O, A, X, I, N, G, S."

"That's a hundred and four plus one twenty-two, and you're up to two twenty-six, just like that," Jorb said. "You know, I never would have even thought of DOLLNICK if I didn't draw the letters in the exact order. Stuff like that happens sometimes, but it doesn't mean anything."

"I'm not putting down a seven-letter word this time," Rinka said, though something in the look she shot the other Drazen implied that it was a matter of choice rather than necessity. "D, R, E, A, M, Y."

"Sixteen," Jorb exhaled, and his whole body sagged in relief that she had stayed on message. "That makes four ninety-six for us."

"Is yoyo hyphenated?" Julie asked Bill.

"Flower?" he relayed the question.

"Yoyo is acceptable with or without a hyphen."

"Flower says it's okay."

"Thirty," Jorb counted up. "Good triple word, and you just broke two hundred and fifty."

"Did you take your letters yet?" Julie asked Rinka.

"Thank you," the choir mistress said, accepting the bag and drawing her tiles. "Oops, we're out. I'm sure you would have caught up otherwise. Right, Jorb?"

The dojo master stared at his rack, his muscles all tense as if he was trying to restrain himself. Then he couldn't hold back any longer and began arranging his tiles around the 'O' that Julie had placed on the triple.

"B, E, L, O, V, E, D, S," he said. "It's only worth sixty-three, but Rinka and I get the points left in your racks because I went out first."

"You don't have to add them all up, Jorb," Julie said. "You more than doubled our score."

"BELOVEDS?" Rinka asked in an unnaturally high voice. "Can somebody have more than one beloved?"

"I don't see why not," Jorb replied before his brain caught up with his mouth, and then he began to stutter. "I muh-muh-mean, not muh-me. Na-na-not at the sa-sa-same time. Wa-wa-wait," he cried as the Drazen girl rose from the table. "I meant not at all."

Rinka grabbed Julie's wrist and dragged her off in the direction of the bathroom again, while Jorb began thumping himself on the head with his tentacle. "Stupid, stupid, stupid. How could I say that? I'm going to the Farling doctor to have my head examined."

"She must know that you didn't mean it," Bill said. "You probably shouldn't have added that bit about 'not at the same time,' though."

"How could he say that?" Rinka demanded of Julie. "Not at the same time? Does he think I'm some sort of mining colony girl looking for a one-night stand?"

"He's just nervous," Julie said. "Bill is always making mistakes like that around me."

"It would have been perfect without the 'S,'" the Drazen girl fumed.

"He couldn't have put it down without using the 'S' in DOLLNICKS," Julie pointed out. "It's not easy finding places for long words at the end of the game."

"DOLLNICKS!" Rinka growled. "DOLLNICKS and BELOVEDS. What's more important to him? Me, or using up all of his letters?"

"I'm sure it's you. Males can't help showing off. Did you see me giving Bill a hard time for putting down COAXINGS? I know he got the word from Flower."

"It was Jorb," the Dollnick AI informed Julie.

"Flower says he got it from Jorb," Julie corrected herself. "You see? Jorb felt so bad about beating us that he helped Bill."

"Really?" Rinka said, her eyes lighting up. "Do you think he meant to say he was coaxing me?"

"Would that be a good thing?"

"Yes. A proper Drazen girl doesn't throw herself at the first suitor to chase her halfway across the galaxy. She has to be coaxed."

"Then I'm sure that's how he meant it. Did Jorb really join Flower because of you?"

"I have a cousin on Union Station who knows somebody who knows somebody who knows somebody in Drazen Intelligence, and that's what I heard," Rinka told her. "I never would have agreed to this otherwise."

"So we should go back before he does something crazy from remorse," Julie said.

"Are you ready for a rematch?" Jorb asked as soon as the girls returned. "We could try different teams."

"I think a different game would be better," Rinka said. "Maybe something with dice."

215

Eighteen

"Trust me on this," Harry said. "Lume loved my last fruitcake, and this one will be better because it's had a couple of weeks to relax."

"But princes tend to be sticklers for tradition, and your recipe may remind him of the modern take on Holiday Loaf with a bit of fruit added in," the Dollnick AI argued. "The safe play would be to stick with alcohol and some vegetable sticks."

"I may not be an interspecies diplomatic consultant, Flower, but I know something about baked desserts. And nobody could mistake my fruitcake for Holiday loaf. There's a lot more fruit than there is cake."

"What's the ultimate shelf life?"

"It depends on how you store them, but the tradition in my family is to wrap the cake in a brandy-soaked cloth and then to put it in a plastic bag and suck out the air."

"With a vacuum pump?"

"With my lungs," Harry said. "Some people store fruit-cakes for years, but I think they're best served at between six to eighteen months. The biggest factor for shelf life is whether you bake with dried fruit or fresh fruit since a higher moisture content will lead to more microbial activity. Of course, with a soaked fruitcake, the alcohol acts as a preservative."

"I'm sure a little ionizing radiation would take care of any microbial problem," Flower told him. "All right. We'll try it your way. Do you want to slice it at the table or should I have Lume do it?"

"Why not Bill?"

"Because Prince Kuerda himself is coming—he must have been visiting the planet on a secret inspection tour. In addition to being one of the wealthiest Dollnick princes, he sits high on the Princely Council. Lume understands court protocol and can help in the negotiations."

"If the Princely Council is the closest thing you have to a government, and Lume is actually undercover for Dollnick Intelligence, doesn't that mean he's working for Prince Kuerda?"

"In a manner of speaking, but he's also working for me, and I pay better bonuses," Flower said. "I sent him to the docking bay to meet the delegation, which arrived a few seconds ago. Your captain and third officer just entered the cafeteria."

The swinging door into the kitchen opened inwards, and Woojin walked through, carrying a wooden crate. He set it down on the counter next to the sink with a grunt. "I'm getting too old to carry around boxes of booze," he said. "Especially in this uniform when I have to be careful of the buttons."

"What is it?" Harry asked.

"Some thousand-year-old Dollnick cactus juice if I understood correctly," Woojin said, fishing out one of the dusty bottles. "Are we supposed to serve it like this, Flower?"

"Rinse it off in the sink, but don't break the seal. Lume will remove the cork at the table."

"Let me do that," Harry offered. "You'll get your sleeves wet." The baker took the bottle from Woojin and rinsed off the dust. "It looks like there's something floating in the bottom of this one," he said. "Maybe we should try a different bottle?"

"That's a Sheezle larva," the Dollnick AI told them. "It's traditional. Just dry the bottle with a towel and put it out. Woojin, the prince will try to stare you down before the negotiations even start. Don't look away, but don't challenge him either. And remember not to speak before him, not even in greeting."

"Got it," Woojin said, winking at Harry and taking the bottle. "Is that cake for us too, or is it only safe for the Dollnicks?"

"It's been soaked in brandy and I need you and Lynx sober for the negotiations. I'll serve the leftovers to the other aliens when they come in for their supper."

Harry picked up the cake and followed the captain out into the small cafeteria where Lynx was examining the place settings that one of the ship's maintenance bots had laid out.

"This dish is solid gold! That goblet too," she said, pointing at the middle setting on the Dollnick side of the table, where three high-seated chairs had been placed to allow the aliens to sit comfortably. "The rest of us got crystal."

"I hope you have the bots do the washing up, Flower," Harry said. "I'd be afraid to drop one of those glasses in the sink, and they look like they're worth a fortune."

"A small fortune," the AI informed them. "They're all from my good set for special occasions. Does everybody understand their instructions?"

"You're not here," Lynx repeated back the main point Flower had drummed into her. "If I need to ask you anything, I'll subvoc. The prince and his aides know that you're present and that Trume Six is your elective stop, but your legal status makes it impossible for them to speak with you directly."

"I have a question," Harry said. "If the Dollnicks agree to your plan and we're here for a week or more, what does that do to the schedule for the rest of the circuit?"

"Our next stop is the midpoint break at Union Station for twelve days, so it doesn't matter if we're late. Anybody who is waiting there to come on board will still get their chance."

"Will our cooperative be able to go down to the surface for a visit here even though it's an alien world? Would it be safe for us?"

"The terraforming project employs millions of human laborers," Flower answered him. "They were brought in for the end of a job that's been going on for hundreds of years, so you'd have no problems with the atmosphere. It's up to the management whether or not they want visitors."

"So these are the workers Jack was talking about that finished the job early."

"Yes, and under the Stryx regulations, at the end of a contract the host species has to pay to either send the workers on to their next job, or to a tunnel network station so they can travel home," Woojin explained. "If we can convince the Dollnicks to release the workers early, Flower is hoping to get them to remain on board."

"She's looking for another twenty thousand people in one chunk?" Harry asked.

"More like two hundred thousand. That's why we'll be here all week if the negotiations pan out. But there's a catch. Did you hear about the attack when we were leaving Bits?"

"We were attacked by pirates?"

"That's what I assumed, and Flower sold the footage to the bunnies. But this morning she admitted that the three attacking ships weren't actually pirates. They were Dollnick mercenary process servers firing across her bow."

"From her court case?"

"That's why she pushed them off rather than destroying them. I should have guessed at the time because Flower doesn't have any patience with real pirates. The point is, Trume Six is in Dollnick space, which means we're in their jurisdiction."

"So you and Lynx are supposedly here negotiating for us, not for her," Harry concluded.

"The prince's representatives would never have agreed to talk directly with me," the Dollnick AI said. "Even without my legal issues, I've been effectively blacklisted for conduct unbecoming a colony ship. It's the reason I went to court in the first place."

"You know, I think I better let Lume slice the cake and I'll sit this one out in the kitchen. This diplomatic stuff is way over my head."

Harry disappeared through the swinging door, and Lynx, resplendent in her third officer's version of the ship's uniform, took her place standing next to her husband and tried to imitate his military posture.

"Are you positive the Dollnick prince will be willing to negotiate with a woman?" she subvoced. "In my experience as a cultural attaché, the diplomats and regular businessmen were willing to talk to me, but a prince?"

"I've already negotiated that in Woojin's name," Flower replied. "It's acceptable because the two of you are married and you handle the family's business affairs."

Lume ushered three Dollnicks into the cafeteria, and after a brief pause in front of Woojin and Lynx, during which not a word was exchanged, the delegation took their seats. Woojin nodded to his wife, and they took the two seats on the other side of the table.

Lume showed the bottle with the larva to the prince and then used a pocket knife to cut off the sealing wax before taking up a Dollnick cork-puller and removing the stopper. He poured a generous shot of the expensive liquor into the gold goblet for the prince, who sniffed it and nodded his approval. Finally, Lume poured smaller amounts for the two other Dollnicks in cut crystal glasses and then went to stand at the end of the table like a sommelier.

Woojin returned the stare of the haughty Dollnick, knowing that if he allowed the prince to establish dominance, negotiations would be short and one-sided. After nearly ten minutes of silence, the prince finally spoke a single word, "Steward."

"I am Durbe, Prince Kuerda's steward on Trume Six," the smallest Dollnick addressed Woojin. "Explain your proposition."

"We understand that the unfamiliarity of some of our contract workers with your processes has led to the work on Trume Six being completed prematurely," Woojin said diplomatically.

"I assure you that the job is on schedule, as are all of our terraforming projects," Durbe replied indignantly. "If you've invited us here for the sake of making insulting accusations, we have nothing further to talk about."

"Forgive my clumsy attempt at speech, I'm just an old military man. My wife is on detached duty as an EarthCent cultural attaché, and I'm sure this meeting would be more productive if she speaks for me."

The prince took a sip from the golden goblet and made a gesture to the steward with one of his lower arms.

"You may proceed," the smaller Dollnick said.

"We're willing to work with you on the narrative, including taking the blame for interfering with your schedule," Lynx offered. "Our mission is to extend whatever help we can to humans living in space, and that includes providing transportation services. We're in a position to offer discounted passage to Union Station for any workers you can part with, and if they agree to stay on board and work through the rest of our circuit, we won't charge anything."

"You're offering free passage?"

"For those who are willing to join the ship, at least for a trial period," Lynx reiterated.

The Dollnick who Woojin had taken for a bodyguard whistled something behind his hand, and the prince made another gesture to the steward.

"How much?" the steward asked.

"We could provide passage to Union Station for just three hundred creds a head," Lynx said, but she was unable to keep the disappointment from her voice since she knew what Flower really wanted was new residents. "If you tell your workers about the opportunities on board—"

"I meant, how much are you willing to pay us per Human?" Durbe interrupted impatiently.

"Pay you? At the expiration of the contract, you have to provide passage for your workers anyway, and that would cost at least double what we're offering."

"But the contract isn't up for another six months on your odd calendar," the steward replied shrewdly. "It's clear you want these Humans for something, and I don't need to tell you that there's a reputational cost to Prince Kuerda if letting them go early is misinterpreted as a scheduling error on our part."

"I've heard that back-dated engineering change-orders can be created to explain any scheduling irregularities," Lume spoke up. "In fact, I understand that since we began employing Human contract laborers, the percentage of large projects completed without late-stage change orders has fallen by more than half."

"I've heard something similar myself," Durbe said, without turning his head away from the humans. "Engineering change orders can certainly explain deviations from the published schedule. Of course, somebody has to pay for the work."

"But the work is already done," Lynx protested.

"The terraforming is done. It's the work of creating the engineering change orders that's expensive. Say a hundred creds a head."

"Let me offer you something to go with your drinks," Lume interjected smoothly, though it was obvious to his fellow Dollnicks that he was buying time for Lynx to communicate with Flower. He lifted the cake dish with his lower set of hands and proceeded in the traditional fashion, slicing with a knife held in one upper hand and removing a wedge with a sterling silver cake server he produced from somewhere. The delegation, all of whom had been sipping their liquor, watched this process closely, and Lume deposited the first slice of heavy cake on the prince's gold plate.

"What do I do?" Lynx subvoced in the meantime. "You didn't say anything about paying."

"Ask him how many Humans we're talking about," Flower instructed over the third officer's implant.

"How many workers do you have who aren't already signed up for a contract somewhere else?" Lynx asked.

The prince raised a forkful of fruitcake to his mouth with one of his upper hands while slipping a lower arm under the table. The steward flinched from the unexpected contact.

"The prince is using tap speech on the steward's leg," Flower reported privately. "There are over four hundred and twenty thousand workers who haven't committed to a new project, but the prince told Durbe to start at a hundred thousand and see how you react."

"I could offer you a hundred thousand at that price, assuming they are willing to go along with it," the steward said. "After all, they are contract workers, not slaves."

The prince took a larger forkful of fruitcake and held it in front of his eyes, seemingly puzzled by the density of different ingredients. Then he moved it into his mouth and nudged the quiet Dollnick, who held his own plate out to Lume.

"I'm not an engineer, but it seems to me that ten million creds would pay for a lot of change orders," Woojin ventured.

"Quadruple the number of Humans and payment due at Union Station," Flower instructed Lynx via her implant.

"As my husband points out, that is quite a lot of money," Lynx said. "While the sum isn't out of the question," she paused to make sure she had the prince's attention, "we had hoped to attract at least four times as many workers. Also, given the, er, inherent dangers of space travel, we keep our ready funds at Union Station."

The steward glanced at his superior, who was now forking fruitcake into his mouth as fast as he could chew, and gave a low whistle to get the prince's attention. Kuerda looked annoyed by the interruption, but he folded the thumb across the pinkie on his upper left hand, poked at an invisible barrier with the three extended fingers, and then curled his fingers into a fist.

"We'd need some sort of premium for the risk you speak of, given that your silent partner recently brushed off a trio of process servers going about their lawful duties," Durbe countered. "Who's to say you'll reach Union Station without encountering an impound fleet?"

"Fiddlesticks," Flower told Lynx. "Four hundred thousand Humans, and a twenty-five cred rebate for every worker who decides to transfer at Union Station. You can throw in a case of that Dollnick tequila. It's over a thousand years old."

"We'll take all of the uncommitted workers you have for ten million if you can come up with four hundred thousand of them," Lynx said. "We'll need to get fifty creds a head back for any of them who leave the ship at Union Station."

"Ridiculous," the prince whistled, speaking directly to the humans for the first time. "If they all transfer, I would end up owing you ten million creds. A twenty-five cred rebate is my best offer, and I'll take this bottle with me."

"You can have a case of it," Lynx said graciously. "Do we have a deal?"

"Wait," the prince said. "Is this cake I've been eating, or some sort of congealed cocktail? I've never had so much alcohol in solid form. What do you call it?"

"Harry's Fruit Cake," Lume replied.

"And where does one shop for such a thing?"

"Ten creds," Flower prompted the third officer over her implant. "And tell him it has an extraordinary shelf life."

"We can sell it for twenty-five creds a cake," Lynx said. "And it keeps forever."

"I'll take all you can make, but I get the monopoly in Dollnick space."

"Deal," Lynx declared.

Prince Kuerda extended both of his lower arms across the table and shook hands with Woojin and Lynx simultaneously.

"You contacted us just as I was preparing to leave Trume Six, and I must be on my way," the prince continued, rising to his feet. "My steward will return to the planet and explain your offer to our contract workers. Accompany us to the docking bay, Lume, and bring the cake. One of you grab the bottle," he added to his aides. "Where's that case?"

"In the kitchen," Woojin said. He brought it out and gave it to the steward. "I guess we'll be hearing from you after you get a chance to talk with the workers."

"I did that as soon as you contacted us," the smallest Dollnick replied smugly. "I kept it to myself as a negotiating tactic. You can start sending down shuttles anytime."

The four Dollnicks exited the cafeteria and Lynx breathed a deep sigh of relief. "That was a lot easier than I thought it would be."

226

"And you're a better negotiator than I expected," Flower said. "How did you know he would go for the higher numbers?"

"I didn't, but I was a trader for ten years, and you develop an instinct for these things. How are you going to get hundreds of thousands of cabins ready in a week?"

"They've been prepared for months now," the Dollnick AI said. "I used bots because there weren't enough people on board to do the work, and when there's a shortage of labor, I keep the biologicals working with food production."

"What if they all stay?' Woojin asked. "Can you really come up with ten million creds when we get to Union Station?"

"If even half of them stay, I'll make my first population milestone, and the bonus will more than cover the cost. Besides, something tells me that Prince Kuerda would accept payment in Harry's Fruit Cakes. Not my first choice for a brand name, but I can work with it."

Nineteen

"When Flower said she may have planted too many fruit trees, she wasn't kidding," Julie said. "Is this whole deck citrus?"

"It's not all oranges, if that's what you mean. There are grapefruits, lemons and limes too," Bill replied.

"Those are all citrus. Didn't she plant any apples, plums or pears?"

"That's the next deck up. She took me and Harry on the grand tour yesterday, and there are three full decks dedicated to fruit, if you include grapes. Flower separated each deck into sections, and she controls the lights and the climate for each section separately, so the trees think they're in different seasons."

"Do trees really think?"

"Razood says that Frunge trees do. There's always a section where the trees are flowering, and there are ape-something bots that help the bees pollinate."

"She probably said apiary bots, and I'm allergic to bees, so don't ask me to go look at them in this dress."

"It looks great on you," Bill said. "You should wear dresses more often."

"I went shopping with Rinka and she picked it out for me," Julie said, but she wondered if Bill would read more into her wearing a dress than she had intended. "I told her I wanted something practical I could wear at work, and she said that this fabric is almost indestructible. It's also guaranteed to be cool in the summer and warm in the winter, if I ever go anywhere with weather again."

"I quit the package delivery business," Bill announced suddenly. "I think Flower only started it because she doesn't have enough to keep herself busy and she likes telling me what to do. And I told Razood I would come in and help whenever he has a big order, but I want to give baking a serious shot, and Harry doesn't have that much time."

"You mean he's too busy to teach you?"

"I mean he's pretty old. Flower is going to make him retire in a few years because the Dollnicks have rules about old people working, but first, she wants him to help set up a commercial baking operation to use up all this fruit."

"So you're quitting delivering packages for Flower to bake fruit cakes for Flower?"

"No. I mean, yes, for now, but I've already told her that once I get good at baking, I want to open my own shop and be my own boss. Harry worked for himself almost his whole career, his wife too."

"His wife worked for him her whole life?"

"For them, like a team. Just think about it."

"Think about Harry and Irene working together?"

"About us. Do you want to work for other people your whole life? We could be partners, just like Harry and Irene. I'll do the baking and you can handle the customers."

Julie hesitated, a dozen answers and excuses jumbled together on her tongue, but in the end, all she could come out with was, "I didn't know you felt that way about me."

"How could you not know? Don't you see the way I look at you?"

"Guys have always—that's not what I meant to say. But we've barely known each other for three months and you're talking about spending our lives together like Harry and Irene. You don't even know me."

"So who knows you better than me, other than Flower? That Zick guy?"

"Is that what this is about? Don't worry, he's with Renée now. They're already living together."

Bill finally stopped walking and surprised Julie by reaching for her hand, the first time she could remember him intentionally touching her skin. "I'm not like those other guys, Julie. You know that Flower gives me advice whether I want it or not, but I also asked Harry and Razood, and they both said I should talk to you. Well, Razood actually said I should have my parents talk to your parents, but you don't have any and I haven't seen my Mom since she remarried. I'm not trying to get you into bed. I just want you to take me seriously as a man, not as some friend who hangs around doing whatever Flower tells him. Can you do that?"

"I'm just surprised is all," Julie said. "I know that Flower wants to stick us together, but I thought you were just going along with it."

"Well I'm not. Caring about you is my idea, and I don't want to wait for some other Zick to come along and then it will be too late. I'm sorry I threw up on your sneakers, but I want to date you, and I want to be able to talk about our future without worrying that you'll think that I'm just saying what Flower tells me to say."

"Okay, Bill. I'd like to try that. But I swapped shifts with Renée at *The Spoon* so I have to get to work. She's probably in a hurry to spend the jump with Zick."

"I'll go with you partway, but I'm meeting with Harry and the captain's wife. We're going to look at one of the industrial decks for the baking business."

"And Flower is planning to hire some of the workers we picked up at this stop to be bakers?"

"I guess there will be all sorts of jobs, from cooking and cleaning up to marketing and package design, not to mention picking fruit," Bill said, as they headed back for the lift tube. "Harry says that commercial baking is as different from working by yourself in a kitchen as taking a bath is from swimming in the ocean."

"Have you ever swum in the ocean?"

"I thought I did once, but then I found out it was just a harbor. The water was salty, though."

"Flower said we can swim on the reservoir deck if we tell her first so she can warn the fish off. I don't think I could."

Bill started laughing.

"What's so funny?" Julie demanded as they entered the lift tube capsule. "Those Dollnick fish are killers."

"Do you realize that Flower hasn't interrupted once since I picked you up at your cabin?"

"She didn't even say anything over your implant?"

"No, you either?"

"No. Food court," Julie instructed the lift tube capsule.

"Do you think she was listening? Maybe she's too busy with getting all of the newcomers settled in. Harry said it amounts to more than doubling the ship's population, though a lot of them will probably leave at Union Station."

"Are you too busy to spy on us, Flower?"

"I don't spy, I supervise, and my Stryx mentor advised me to give you more room," the Dollnick AI replied immediately.

"Attention all shoppers," the captain's voice announced. "We will be departing Trume Six in forty-five minutes. Visitors who fail to disembark on time will be charged the cost of passage to our next destination at commercial rates and be subject to ship's law. This is your final warning."

"Quiet shift for me," Julie commented. "I'll probably spend most of my time restocking and doing prep." She looked at Bill out of the corner of her eye, and added, "I can give you a free coffee if you stop by."

"Deal," Bill said, breaking into a smile.

The doors slid open and the girl exited, and then without instructions, the capsule started off again. After picking up Lynx and Harry, Flower brought the three of them to Deck Forty.

"I've had my bots transferring equipment from some of the kitchens at the other end of the ship," the Dollnick AI explained. "It's all very preliminary."

"Why couldn't we just do the baking in those unused kitchens?" Bill asked.

"Efficiency," Harry explained. "Commercial baking is like running a factory assembly line with food as the product. Since we're working with crops grown on board that need to be processed into ingredients, it adds a layer of complication that I've never had to deal with. Flower has had plenty of experience grinding wheat and making sugar for five million Dollnicks so I'm not going to worry about it."

"I'm sure that I'll find some good candidates to train up for operations management in our haul from Trume Six," Flower said. "My reason for bringing you all the way down here is to help you make the linkage between the recipes you develop and the processes that will turn them into saleable products. You and Bill will be working in

232

dessert research. We're going to launch with a line of fruitcakes because I know Prince Kuerda will buy our production, and I have a bumper crop of fruit to harvest that's only going to get bigger. Ultimately, I'll adjust what I grow according to demand, both on-board consumption and in the packaged food market."

"How many of the new workers do you think you can find jobs for?" Lynx asked.

"All of them," Flower replied, as the lift tube doors opened. "On my last real mission, there were over a hundred thousand Dollnick colonists employed on this deck in a micro-weaving operation. They took the equipment with them."

"I have a hard time picturing all those Dollnicks working at manual labor," Harry said. "I thought that's why they hired so many of us."

"Did you think every member of an advanced species can be a scientist or a poet, or even that they want to be?" the ship's AI challenged the baker. "Take Lume. He runs a lunch counter."

"But that's just a cover job so he can work as an intelligence agent."

"Ask him sometime. He was on the verge of taking early retirement to become a street food vendor when this opportunity to combine his passions came up. And most of the other Dollnicks on board work in the distribution business. Do you think selling Gem nanobots and Verlock magnetic bearing replacements in bulk is that different from weighing out nails or mixing paint?"

"What is that thing?" Bill asked, pointing at a giant oval machine with a short section of exposed conveyor belt.

"It looks like a commercial dishwasher for a banquet facility," Harry said. "A single person can stack dirty dishes in the racks as they pass and take clean ones when they come back out. But I've never seen one so big, or with so much of the track enclosed."

"That, my Human employees, is the pinnacle of Dollnick food preparation technology," Flower said proudly. "It can do everything from mixing dough and baking bread to shelling nuts and grinding flour. It has the temperature range to make ice cream or melt aluminum, and as Harry guessed, it can also wash the dishes. They're popular on colony ships as a backup for manual labor in case of emergencies."

"But I thought your goal was to employ as many people as possible."

"You're correct. I just wanted you to see the machine before I had the bots reconfigure it into a linear oven for the fruitcake production line. We'll start with a hundred and take it from there."

"A hundred ovens?" Lynx asked. "How many people will that employ? Ten? Twenty?"

"How long would it take you to walk from where you're standing to the next structural spoke?"

"I guess a couple minutes. What does that have to do with anything?"

"Given the speed of the conveyer and the required baking time for Harry's current recipe, the linear ovens I've designed will just fit between two spokes," Flower said. "I expect that each oven will require at least twenty workers preparing the ingredients, mixing the batter and pouring it into molds, and another ten workers on the other end boxing the finished product. That doesn't count the office staff, warehouse employees, quality control, sales support, and of course, research and development. I estimate that each linear oven will employ fifty workers per shift, or over a hundred and ten if we run around the clock."

"Why not a hundred and fifty?" Lynx asked.

"Sales support, research and development, and some of the office tasks will only work one shift. Now, let's take a look at the printing operation."

By the time Flower finished showing off her nascent fruitcake factory, the countdown to entering the tunnel had begun. Lynx and Harry headed back to their cabins to sleep through the disconcerting transition to hyperspace, and Bill headed for *The Spoon*. When he got there, Julie was nowhere to be seen, but he took a stool at the counter. He noticed a napkin with some printing on it draped over the register, and after a guilty look around to see if anybody was watching, he snagged it and puzzled out the scrawl.

Took one coffee to go and the last plain donut – Capt. Pyun.

"Flower?" Bill asked. "Doesn't the captain usually come down and inspect the food court right after he makes his final announcement?"

"He visited the food court thirty-two minutes ago," the AI confirmed. "Why do you ask?"

"Julie's not here and the captain left a note about owing her for a coffee. I'm sure she would have seen it."

"Maybe she's in the restroom?"

"For a half-hour?"

"That would be excessive for her. Oh, this isn't good."

"What isn't good?" Bill demanded.

"I can't locate her."

"Try her implant."

"That's what I'm doing. I had the Farling doctor give you both high-end models. It's extremely unlikely that it's failed."

"But everybody said that she's safe now, that the contract on her life was cancelled," Bill shouted at the ship's AI, even though he knew his implant could pick up whispers and subvocalizations. Unwilling to take the time to go around, he climbed over the counter to make sure Julie wasn't lying dead on the floor. "If she's not here, where is she? Did you leave her behind on that Dollnick world?"

"I watch the arrivals and departures and I would have seen her," Flower said. "Don't panic, she must be here somewhere."

"You're the one who said it's not good."

"The walk-in freezer."

"What?"

"The restaurants in this area of the food court share a walk-in freezer. It's behind the soft serve."

"She's in there?" Bill asked as he ran out from behind the counter heading for the soft serve. "Why can't you contact her?"

"When the door is closed it's a Faraday cage. Lume needed somewhere private he could interview his agents without me listening in."

"Where is it?" he shouted again, skidding to a halt behind the soft serve. "Shouldn't there be a big metal door?"

"Somebody added that corkboard so local businesses could post help-wanted ads—the turnover in food service is unbelievable."

"Where's the handle?" Bill cried in frustration.

"It's at Dollnick height."

"Can't you just open it?"

"I didn't want to compromise the safety features. Freezers can be quite dangerous. Don't close the door behind you and I'll be able to access her implant."

Bill finally located the push-button handle next to a solicitation for second-shift fry cooks that paid better than either of his current jobs, and wrapping his fingers around the handle, depressed the button with his thumb and pulled the door open. The freezer was huge, but he only had eyes for the girl on the floor. Julie was lying flat on her back, limbs askew, a mop lying across her stomach.

"Send the doctor," Bill cried. "She's lying on her back and she's not moving." He raced forward to place his fingers on her throat and check for a pulse like he had seen in dramas, but her skin felt cold to the touch. "She's cold, and I can't feel a pulse."

"Her heartbeat is a bit low, but her implant doesn't report any major systems failures," the Dollnick AI told him. "Try to wake her up and get her out of the freezer."

"I'm not a doctor, but I know you aren't supposed to move people who might have a spinal injury."

"Her implant would show a problem with the nervous system if that were the case. It's all tied together in your species."

Bill placed both hands on her face and started patting her cheeks, not having the heart to try a real slap. "Julie! Wake up!"

"Try kissing her," Flower advised.

"I'm not kissing Julie while she's passed out on the floor," he shouted. "Sometimes your advice really sucks."

"I think it would be sort of romantic," Julie muttered, her eyes fluttering open. "Better than having you pat my cheeks like you're making a hamburger. What happened?"

"You weren't at the counter when I came, and there was a note from the captain he must have left a half-hour ago. Flower suggested looking for you in the freezer."

"I remember now," Julie said, levering herself up on an elbow despite Bill begging her to just wait for the doctor. "I dropped the container of soup I was putting away to freeze and it all spilled out. It must have frozen while I went back to the diner to get the mop. I slipped and my leg shot up over my head just like the funny little guy I saw on movie night at the independent living cooperative. What was his name?"

"Charlie Chaplin," Flower said. "Move her out of there and close the door before all of the ice cream melts. I'll send a bot to clean up."

"I still think we should wait for the doctor," Bill said, but Julie had a grip on his shoulder and pulled herself to an upright sitting position.

"I'm freezing. Help me up and get me out of here."

Bill put his hands under her arms and straightened up with her, bringing them both to their feet. Julie wrapped her arms around his neck and sagged against him. He began half-carrying, half-walking her to the door. Some sort of orchestral piece began to play over his implant.

"What's going on?" he asked. "Can you hear that, Julie?"

"I asked Flower for music to get you over your fear of slow dancing," Julie told him. "You really should learn to subvoc."

"I'm waiting for you to offer to teach me. Are you really okay?"

"Just cold, and you're warm. I never knew you were so warm. Dance me back to *The Spoon* and I'll be fine."

Bill wanted to argue, but not enough to risk her letting go of him, so he focused on shuffling back the way they came, trying to move in rhythm with the music, but not having much success. By the time they reached the open area of tables in front of the diner, Julie was no longer using him to stay upright, and he wasn't sure which of them was leading.

"My lips really are numb," she mumbled, turning her face towards his.

"Kiss her, you fool," Flower practically shouted over Bill's implant.

Bill tilted his head a little and moved his face closer, closing his eyes and puckering up self-consciously. Just before their lips touched, a loud voice interrupted.

"All right, then. Enough of that. Break it up and let me get a look."

The young people opened their eyes and saw the Farling doctor towering over them, rubbing away on his speaking legs.

"If it isn't the spy who came in from the cold, except neither of you have been recruited by an intelligence service yet, have you? Any dizziness, confusion, numbness in your arms or legs?"

"I'm just cold," Julie protested. "I must have been in the freezer for half an hour."

"Think of it as thirty extra minutes of life you'll get before you spoil," the doctor said, and brandished an alien-looking device in front of Julie's face. "Don't move around while I'm measuring you," he instructed. After a few seconds, he shoved the portable scanner back in his medical bag and pulled out a small flashlight, which he shined in her eyes. "Have you noticed anything funny, Flower?"

"No. As far as the implant is concerned, she's functioning normally."

"What's the square root of seventeen?" M793qK demanded. "Don't tell her, Bill."

"A little more than four?" Julie ventured.

"Her brain is in better shape than ninety percent of the Humans I see," the doctor concluded. "Carry on with what you were doing, but keep your clothes on or you'll ruin my appetite. And first, somebody pour me a Deck Three vodka, stat."

Twenty

"Sorry I can only stay for a few minutes," Bill told Razood. "I'm helping Harry with the wedding cake and then I have to change. How come you aren't dressed for work?"

"I am dressed for work." The Frunge blacksmith was wearing a metallic suit the apprentice had never seen, and stood ramrod straight behind the table displaying his finest wares. "Business isn't all about swinging a hammer, you know. Quick, put on that cloak."

"This?" Bill asked, retrieving a fashionable cloak from the peg where his leather apron normally hung. "Do you always dress up when we're stopped at Union Station?"

"Just put it on. And hurry, he's coming out of the candle-making shop."

Bill felt a little foolish throwing the cloak over his shoulders, and he fumbled with the clasp. When he looked up, an oddly-shaped robot that could best be described as a barrel with treads floated up to the table and extended a pincer to heft one of Razood's swords.

"Fine work, but I recognize it from the last time you stopped here," the robot announced. "It doesn't look like your prime inventory is moving, but you still have the excess funds to hire help?"

"My apprentice," the Frunge answered respectfully. "He's been working for me a couple of months as a part-time trial, but it looks like I'm going to lose him to Flower's new food business. I'm sure you know that Humans work cheap."

"Not if you take into account how much they cost you in raw materials, patent filings and marketing promotions."

"Bill mainly pumps the bellows, Stryx Jeeves."

"Then you're lucky. How many sets of books do you have for me to inspect this time?"

"I started paying Flower to keep all of my records," Razood replied. "She gets the data straight from my mini-register."

"I don't suppose you're doing a cash business on the side?"

"Who uses cash these days?"

"Who indeed," Jeeves muttered, setting down the sword and pointing with his pincer. "What's that supposed to be?"

"The four-headed axe? It's a custom order from some Human game developers—"

"Stop right there, I know the type, and I understand that Flower picked up a large contingent of them on Bits. Does this mean that you won't require a subsidy going forward?"

"The weapons they buy are just toys, it doesn't pay like real craftsmanship," Razood said apologetically. "I only accept their commissions because I know how enthusiastic Flower is about keeping these new Humans on board."

"Yes, to make her population milestones," Jeeves said. "You're set for another circuit, but if you haven't started making a profit by then, I'm going to ask Frunge Intelligence to find somebody with more business sense to run the smithy."

Razood remained at attention while the young Stryx floated off towards the lift tubes, and his apprentice kept the silence until the robot was out of sight.

"That was the Stryx who sponsors Colonial Jeevesburg?" Bill asked incredulously. "Flower's maintenance bots are twice his size and have four times as many arms."

"With the Stryx, it's what you don't see that matters," Razood explained. "The robot bodies are just something the young ones put on to go out and mix with the biological species, but they've got the whole multiverse figured out."

"And he cares how you dress for work?"

"I only wear this when we visit Union Station, and your cloak is from his fashion brand."

"I'm sorry about you losing the subsidy after this circuit."

"Jeeves says the same thing every time we stop at Union Station," Razood told Bill. "He's never pulled a subsidy from any of the shops in Colonial Jeevesburg yet. Besides, it's all pocket change compared to what they're going to have to pay Flower for making her first population milestone."

"A half-million people living on board is a lot."

"She's still only at ten percent capacity."

A woman dressed in a hoopskirt who Bill recognized as the proprietress of the millinery shop called to them as she passed by. "Come on, or you'll be late for the post-audit party. Flower sent complimentary pies with fresh fruit fillings."

"How hard is it for them to remember that I don't do crust," Razood complained to Bill. "Besides, I see some Hortens from Union Station heading this way. One of them

243

bought a sword from me yesterday and promised he'd return with his friends. You better get going and I'll see you later."

Three decks away, Jeeves entered the alien cafeteria where he had arranged to conduct the Stryx audit of Flower's milestone achievements. The captain and Lynx were waiting along with Lume, Brenda from the independent living cooperative, and the Farling doctor.

"I see you brought in the heavy hitters," Jeeves communicated electronically to the Dollnick ship's AI. "Does that mean you expect problems?"

"Allow me to introduce my new legal representative," Flower responded out loud. "Brenda, this is Jeeves."

"Pleased to meet you," Brenda said nervously, and reflexively extended a hand. Jeeves grasped it gently with his pincer and gave it a shake before pivoting to the pair of aliens.

"Gone native, M793qK?" the young Stryx inquired.

"Business is good, and I've learned to value the relative privacy after my years on Union Station," the Farling replied. "Flower invited me to attend this audit as an observer because I'm thinking about putting in for a Stryx research grant on Human longevity. I want to find out how hard it is to collect milestone bonuses."

"And you?" Jeeves asked Lume.

"Moral support, but it's almost time for dinner, so I would have been here in a few minutes anyway."

"Then I'll try to get through this as quickly as possible so it won't interfere with your dining pleasure. My elders informed me that you put in a claim for your first population milestone, Flower. I've counted the qualified Humans on board, and the number I come up with is approximately seventeen thousand less than your stated total."

"If I may," Brenda said. "I've read a translation of the contract in question, and based on the difference you just pointed out, it appears to me that you're treating the boarding school population as transients."

"Because they are transients. Temporary residents shall be defined as persons who have joined the ship's complement for a short time only," Jeeves quoted the contract. "That would make them transients."

"But how can you say that boarding school students have joined for a short time only? Some of them have been continuously on board for three years, and the younger students may end up remaining here for a decade, longer if Flower starts a branch campus of the Open University."

"But they have a home to return to," Jeeves argued. "We're talking about legal minors by Human definition. Their parents haven't given up custody to Flower."

"Their parents should have read the fine print of my boarding school contracts," the Dollnick AI interjected.

"Approximately five thousand of the students are over sixteen, which is the age of majority on CoSHC worlds," Brenda countered. "And if you're taking Earth precedence into account, there's a legal difference between permanent residency and domicile, where permanent residency implies a non-temporary home, and domicile is a permanent home, such as where military or diplomatic personnel may return after retirement."

"Isn't this normally where you project a hologram of dense text and tell us to read the fine print?" Lynx teased Jeeves.

"I could do that, but I don't understand why you're arguing. Flower claimed five hundred and twenty thousand Human residents, and my count makes it five hundred and three thousand, give or take the odd vagrant.

The workers from Trume Six who announced they were getting off at Union Station have already departed, and considering that you're leaving in less than twelve hours, I think that it's a safe bet she's made the milestone in any case."

"Then that's done and we don't have to discuss it any further," Woojin declared. "I'm performing a wedding later and I invited Joe to come and take a look around before we leave. Is he on board yet, Flower?"

"The EarthCent ambassador's husband arrived five minutes ago and I've routed him to this location," the Dollnick AI responded. "Make sure to send him home with a box of fresh fruit."

"We have plenty of fresh fruit on Union Station," Jeeves pointed out.

"Free fresh fruit?"

"If that's how you do business, you're going to go through your fifty million cred bonus long before you make the next milestone."

"Fifty million creds!" Lynx exclaimed. "That's like a hundred creds a head for every human on board."

"Which is why I was prepared to meet Prince Kuerda's original offer," Flower said smugly. "Thanks to your negotiating assistance, I expect to get away with paying him two hundred thousand fruit cakes when all is said and done. Now all I need is a cheap source for a few thousand barrels of good brandy, if anybody has any ideas."

"I'm not sure I want to know what you're talking about," Jeeves said, spinning around. "Sorry about yesterday's poker game, Woojin, but you owed me from last time."

"Why wasn't I invited to the poker game?" Flower demanded. "I could have sent a bot to play for me again."

"Lynx thought you'd be too busy with the audits," Woojin lied. "Hello, Joe," he greeted his friend.

"Wooj," the older man acknowledged, and then reclaimed a plastic crate from the bot Flower had sent to guide him. "Thanks for the help," he said to the bot, and then offered the crate to the Farling. "As promised."

"Thank you, Joe," M793qK said. "Just what the doctor ordered. The canned beer that they sell on this ship doesn't hold a candle to your homebrew. How much do I owe you?"

"It's on the house, Doc. I've got a fine son-in-law thanks to your medical intervention, and I hear that Clive's sister and nephew are doing well also." Joe looked around the cafeteria and laughed. "When Flower's bot said it was bringing me to the nerve center of the ship, I assumed it meant the bridge. You look familiar," he added, offering a hand to Lume.

"I worked undercover a few times at your training camp posing as an unemployed actor helping your agents understand Dollnick culture," Lume replied. "Sorry about the deception."

"Comes with the territory," Joe said. "I hope you taught our agents the proper way to ask directions to the bathroom. We had to fire a Horten actor on that account."

"I like to think I earned my pay."

"If you're done with us, Flower, we should get to the pre-wedding party," Woojin said. "The ceremony isn't for another thirty minutes, but I don't want to make them nervous."

"Wait. Could I ask you a favor, Joe?" the Dollnick AI inquired.

"Try me," the EarthCent ambassador's husband said.

"Beowulf should have the ability to identify foods that the Cayl will enjoy. I want him to taste a fruit cake for me before I try marketing in their empire."

"Sure, just get it to me before I return to Union Station and I'll let you know what he thinks. But if it's like any other fruit cake I've had, the alcohol content will be too high for the Cayl to issue it as field rations."

"I intend to market the fruitcake for holiday consumption only. I'll have it wrapped and waiting for you when you leave," Flower promised. "Don't forget your hat, Woojin, or the wedding won't be official."

"What was all that about?" Joe asked his old commanding officer as Jeeves led the way to the nearest lift tube.

"Apparently Flower has decided that the future lies in packaged foods, and in addition to being popular with the aliens, alcohol-soaked fruit cakes have an excellent shelf life," Woojin said. "Flower got the idea from a baker who joined at our last Earth stop intending to retire. He lost his savings in a scam and she hired him to cook for the alien spies who eat in the small cafeteria we were just in."

"You've got an interesting command."

"If you can call it that. My main duties seem to be making announcements over the public address system and performing weddings, though to tell you the truth, I've got no complaints. Lynx works a lot harder than I do keeping track of the business activity on board. Flower didn't even tell me until after the fact when some mercenary process-servers fired across her bow in an attempt to deliver her a Dollnick court summons."

"I can imagine how well that worked out," Joe said with a laugh. "Why didn't Lynx come with us?"

"She's stopping home to pick up Em. We couldn't find a sitter and Flower sent a bot."

"I'll mention it to Donna's girls when I get back. Maybe they'll expand InstaSitter beyond the Stryx stations."

"That would mean having Flower do the back office and monitoring work that Libby does for InstaSitter on Union Station," Jeeves pointed out.

Woojin and Joe exchanged a look, and the EarthCent ambassador's husband decided that trying to expand the babysitting service to the Dollnick colony ship probably wasn't the best idea he'd had.

"You're here," Julie greeted the captain when the two men and Stryx Jeeves entered the small room at the back of the improvised wedding hall. "I can't believe how nervous I am."

"You look lovely," Woojin told her.

"The groom is one lucky man," Joe agreed.

"At first, I thought he was too old to get married again, but he's in great shape for his age, and why shouldn't he have another chance for happiness?" Julie said. Then she pointed at her ear for a moment and added, "The bouquet is here. I'll be right back."

"Just how old is the groom?" Joe asked after the girl ran out.

"Well, he did two full contracts on Dollnick ag worlds, and a stint as an independent trader, so I'd guess in his early seventies," Woojin said.

"Is he rich?"

"I think he has a pension from the second Dollnick contract. Why do you ask?"

"Isn't she around five decades too young for him?"

"Five decades too young for whom?" Nancy announced her presence. The off-white gown she was wearing looked suspiciously like it had been stored in a garment bag for the last fifty years. "And who are your friends, Captain?"

"Joe McAllister and Stryx Jeeves. Joe served under me in the mercenaries and he thought that Julie was the bride."

"We'll have a problem if she is since I've already moved my things into Jack's cabin. We're going to keep mine empty and use it as an office for the cooperative."

Julie reentered the room with the flowers and announced, "Bill and Harry just brought the cake in so you can start any time."

"You carry the bouquet," Nancy told her. "Your skin holds up to the contrast better than mine."

"Let me ping Lynx," Woojin said. "She'll be mad if I start without her."

"She's here," Julie told him. "I saw her with your daughter. They're sitting right in the front."

"I'm too old to wait a minute longer than I have to," Nancy said. "Anybody who can't show up twenty minutes early for a wedding is just coming for the food, so they won't miss anything. Somebody cue the Barry Girls."

Julie ran out again and signaled the three sisters who had joined Flower's Paradise at Timble. The trio began playing Mendelssohn's wedding march on a violin, viola, and cello. Julie returned with Bill, who looked like he had been hastily stuffed into a borrowed set of clothes.

"Are you sure Jack wants me as best man?" he asked. "I've only met him once."

"I'm not walking down the aisle with just a bouquet for company," Julie told him. "You said you wanted to date me, so man up."

"Here are the rings, dear," Nancy said, handing Bill two gold bands. "Just keep your fist closed until Woojin asks for them and they won't get lost. I believe you're supposed to be up front waiting for us, Captain."

"Right, I'll see you there," Woojin said. He made his way quickly around the seated guests to stand next to Jack, who was waiting all alone at the front of the common room, looking rather paler than usual.

"You two go quick before the music runs out," Nancy told the young people. "And you, what was your name again?"

"Joe. Sorry to crash your wedding, but—"

"I like your suit. You're walking me down the aisle."

"My daughter made it for me," Joe said, offering Nancy his arm. "I'm guessing you didn't have a rehearsal."

"You guess correctly," the bride said, setting off with measured steps. When they reached the end of the aisle, she let go of her escort's arm and went to stand on the other side of Woojin. Joe took the open seat between Lynx and where Jeeves was floating.

"From time immemorial, the greatest privilege granted to a ship's captain is that of binding a couple in holy matrimony," Woojin began. "We are gathered here today to witness the beginning of a new life for Nancy and Jack, who requested I keep the ceremony short because they want to maximize the time they have left to spend together. Bill, do you have the rings?"

Bill pulled a white-knuckled fist out of his pocket and opened his cramped fingers over Woojin's palm.

"Nancy, Jack. Please take your partner's ring and place it on their ring finger," the captain continued, and then waited for the couple to comply. "Do you, Jack, take Nancy to be your lawful wedded wife?"

"I do," Jack said.

"Do you, Nancy, take Jack to be your lawful wedded husband?"

251

"I do," the former schoolteacher answered in a ringing voice.

"Then by the power vested in me by EarthCent and by wearing this hat, I now pronounce you man and wife. That's as short as I can make it, and you may kiss the bride."

As Jack bent down to kiss his petite wife, the Barry Girls started playing a popular tune that everybody recognized, though nobody knew the words. When Nancy came up for air, she told Julie, "Throw the bouquet. I don't want to spend my wedding night with a rotator cuff injury."

Julie searched the audience for the youngest unmarried female, and settling on Brenda, threw the bouquet directly at her. It came to a dead stop at the top of the arc, then reversed course and came right back at the young woman.

"Are you doing this, Flower?" Julie demanded, dodging to the side. "It's not funny."

"I think it's kind of funny, and it demonstrates excellent control of manipulation fields for a Dollnick AI," Jeeves commented to Lynx. "Libby told me that Flower needed some matchmaking advice and asked me to stop by in my capacity as a former troubleshooter for the Eemas dating service. Flower's instincts are good, but her approach is a little too muscular. Still, I'd say the experiment is a success."

"What experiment?" Woojin asked, joining the group.

"The question was never whether Flower could assist Humans, it was whether humanity had anything to offer Flower in return. It's not my decision, but based on what I've seen, I'm sure my elders will extend the operating subsidy beyond the current contract."

"With all of her new businesses, she may not need—" Woojin paused and pointed at his ear. "Flower insists I state that my views are my own and do not reflect the opinions of this colony ship."

"Do me a favor and grab the bouquet," Julie begged Bill. "Flower isn't answering me and I look like an idiot with a bunch of pink and white roses following me around."

"I'll catch them, but first I want you to agree to a real date, with dancing and a goodnight kiss," Bill said. "And we both get Flower to promise not to listen in or offer advice."

"Done," Julie agreed.

"Too muscular my foot," Flower transmitted to Jeeves triumphantly. "I'm the one who taught Bill to negotiate like that. You can tell my mentor that everything is going according to plan."

From the Author

You can help keep Flower open for business even if you were born too early to grab the space elevator up for her next stop at Earth to shop in the bazaar. Tell a friend about **Independent Living** and the **Union Station** series.

If you like science fiction without wars, you should also enjoy my AI Diaries trilogy, which starts on present-day Earth with **Turing Test**. You can sign up for e-mail notification of my new releases on the **IfItBreaks.com** website or find me on Facebook.

About the Author

E. M. Foner lives in Northampton, MA with an imaginary German Shepherd who's been trained to bite central bankers. The author welcomes reader comments at e_foner@yahoo.com.

Other books by the author:

Independent Living

Date Night on Union Station

Alien Night on Union Station

High Priest on Union Station

Spy Night on Union Station

Carnival on Union Station

Wanderers on Union Station

Vacation on Union Station

Guest Night on Union Station

Word Night on Union Station

Party Night on Union Station

Review Night on Union Station

Family Night on Union Station

Book Night on Union Station

LARP Night on Union Station

Career Night on Union Station

Last Night on Union Station

Soup Night on Union Station

Meghan's Dragon

Turing Test

Human Test

Magic Test

255

Made in the USA
Middletown, DE
10 December 2019